MOTHER'S BIBLE

A GUIDEBOOK FOR EVERY MOTHER

UTTARAYAN DEB

Made with ♥ on the Notion Press Platform
www.notionpress.com

Dedicated to a lovely Mother:

PRITHA

Contents

Preface

In a world that constantly presents new challenges and opportunities for growth, the role of a mother remains a cornerstone of guidance, support, and love in a child's life. Each day, mothers around the world strive to give their children the tools they need to thrive physically, emotionally, cognitively, and socially. Yet, the path to raising a well-rounded child is often filled with questions, concerns, and a longing for dependable knowledge. *The Mother's Bible* has been crafted as a comprehensive guidebook to address these needs, offering mothers the insights and resources they need to navigate this journey.

This book seeks to empower mothers by addressing every aspect of a child's development, from infancy through the early years. We understand that the foundation laid in a child's earliest years has a lasting impact on their life. Thus, each chapter is designed to serve as a practical guide to help mothers foster not only their child's physical health but also their cognitive growth, emotional resilience, social skills, and ethical understanding.

In the pages that follow, you will find guidance on essentials like nutrition, health, and wellness, along with milestones in physical and cognitive development. These sections are balanced with insights into emotional and social development, behavior management, and the importance of routines, helping to ensure your child grows in a nurturing and structured environment.

Recognizing that every child's journey is unique, we have included dedicated sections on special needs and inclusivity to help mothers embrace diversity and understand developmental differences. Additionally, our chapter on parental self-care reminds mothers of the importance of their own well-being, underscoring that a healthy, balanced parent is crucial to raising a thriving child.

We believe that a mother's influence goes beyond the walls of her home, shaping the next generation's values, ethics, and openness to cultural diversity. Our section on cultural and ethical values encourages mothers to instil these principles in their children, building a foundation of respect and empathy.

The Mother's Bible is intended to be more than just a guidebook; it is a companion that grows with you and your child. It's our hope that each section provides clarity, encouragement, and practical advice, supporting mothers as they nurture a bright, compassionate, and resilient future generation.

Thank you for choosing *The Mother's Bible* as a part of your parenting journey. May it serve as a source of guidance, strength, and inspiration, helping you navigate the wonderful and rewarding adventure of motherhood.

With heartfelt appreciation,
Uttarayan Deb

ONE

INTRODUCTION

Importance of Early Childhood Development

Early childhood development (ECD) refers to the physical, cognitive, social, and emotional growth that occurs in children from birth to around eight years of age. This period is critical as it lays the foundation for a child's overall well-being and future potential.

Brain Development:

During early childhood, the brain develops at an unparalleled rate, forming neural connections that shape a child's learning and behaviour. Research has shown that by the age of three, a child's brain has reached 80% of its adult size. The experiences a child encounters during this period, whether positive or negative, have lasting impacts on brain architecture. Proper stimulation, love, and nurturing contribute to healthy brain development, enhancing cognitive abilities like problem-solving, memory, and language.

Social and Emotional Growth:

Early childhood is also crucial for social and emotional development. Children learn to form relationships, manage emotions, and develop empathy. These skills are fundamental for building resilience, a key factor in coping with life's challenges. Positive interactions with caregivers, especially mothers, foster a sense of security and trust, which are vital for healthy social and emotional development.

Physical Development:

The physical growth of children in their early years is rapid, encompassing motor skills, coordination, and overall health. Proper nutrition, physical activity, and sleep are essential components that contribute to a child's physical development. A well-nourished and active child is more likely to develop strong bones, muscles, and a healthy immune system, which are necessary for preventing illnesses and supporting overall growth.

Impact on Future Success:

The quality of early childhood development significantly influences a child's future success. Children who receive adequate support in their early years are more likely to excel academically, socially, and emotionally. They tend to have better health outcomes, higher educational attainment, and improved economic stability in adulthood. Conversely, a lack of proper early development can lead to long-term challenges, including lower academic achievement, behavioural issues, and poorer health.

The Role of the Environment:

The environment in which a child grows plays a pivotal role in early development. Factors such as family stability, access to education, healthcare, and community resources contribute to shaping a child's development. Supportive environments that provide enriching experiences, emotional security, and educational opportunities foster optimal growth. Conversely, adverse conditions like poverty, neglect, or exposure to violence can hinder development, making early intervention crucial.

Role of Mothers in Child Development

Mothers play a central role in the development of their children, often serving as the primary caregivers during the early years. Their influence extends beyond basic care, encompassing emotional, cognitive, and social aspects of a child's growth.

Nurturing and Emotional Support:

A mother's love and affection are foundational to a child's emotional well-being. Consistent nurturing helps children develop a secure attachment, which is vital for building self-esteem and confidence. Securely attached children are more likely to explore their environment, engage in learning, and form healthy relationships later in life. Mothers who are emotionally responsive to their children's needs, providing comfort and support, help their children learn to regulate their emotions and cope with stress.

Cognitive Stimulation:

Mothers often serve as their children's first teachers, introducing them to language, numbers, and concepts through everyday interactions. Reading, talking, and playing with children stimulate cognitive development, enhancing their language skills, memory, and problem-solving abilities. Mothers who engage in these activities foster a love for learning and curiosity in their children, laying the groundwork for future academic success.

Health and Nutrition:

Mothers are typically responsible for ensuring that their children receive proper nutrition and health care. They play a critical role in establishing healthy eating habits, which are crucial for physical growth and development. Educating mothers about the importance of balanced diets, breastfeeding, and regular medical check-ups can significantly impact a child's health outcomes. Moreover, mothers who prioritize their children's physical activity contribute to their motor skill development and overall well-being.

Role Modelling:

Children often learn by observing the behaviour of their mothers. A mother's actions, attitudes, and values profoundly influence her child's development. For example, a mother who demonstrates kindness, empathy, and patience models these qualities for her child. Similarly, a mother who values education and hard work instils these principles in her child, shaping their attitudes toward learning and perseverance.

Social and Moral Development:

Mothers also guide their children's social and moral development, teaching them how to interact with others, understand social norms, and develop a sense of right and wrong. Through everyday interactions, mothers help children learn to share, cooperate, and resolve conflicts. They also play a key role in instilling moral values, such as honesty, respect, and responsibility, which are essential for becoming socially responsible adults.

Support for Mothers:

While mothers play a crucial role in child development, it is important to recognize the need for support systems. Parenting, especially in the early years, can be challenging, and mothers benefit from support from their families, communities, and society at large. Providing mothers with resources, education, and emotional support can empower them to fulfil their roles effectively, ultimately benefiting the development of their children.

TWO
NUTRITION

Essential Nutrients for Growing Children

Proper nutrition is vital for a child's growth, development, and overall health. During childhood, the body requires a range of essential nutrients to support the rapid physical and cognitive development that occurs during this period.

Macronutrients:

- **Carbohydrates:** Carbohydrates are the primary source of energy for children. They fuel physical activity and support brain function. Whole grains, fruits, and vegetables are excellent sources of complex carbohydrates, providing sustained energy and essential nutrients like fibre.
- **Proteins:** Proteins are the building blocks of the body, crucial for growth, tissue repair, and immune function. Children need sufficient protein to support muscle development, organ function, and the production of enzymes and hormones. High-quality protein sources include lean meats, fish, eggs, dairy products, beans, and legumes.
- **Fats:** Fats are essential for brain development, hormone production, and the absorption of fat-soluble vitamins (A, D, E, and K). Healthy fats, such as those found in avocados, nuts, seeds, and olive oil, should be included in a child's diet. Omega-3 fatty acids, found in fatty fish like salmon, are particularly important for brain health.

Micronutrients:

- **Vitamins:**
    - **Vitamin A:** Important for vision, immune function, and skin health. It can be found in foods like carrots, sweet potatoes, and spinach.
    - **Vitamin C:** Supports immune function and aids in the absorption of iron. Citrus fruits, strawberries, and bell peppers are excellent sources.
    - **Vitamin D:** Essential for bone health and calcium absorption. Sunlight exposure and foods like fortified milk, eggs, and fatty fish provide vitamin D.
    - **B Vitamins:** These vitamins support energy production and nervous system function. Whole grains, eggs, meat, and leafy greens are good sources.
    - **Vitamin E:** Acts as an antioxidant, protecting cells from damage. It can be found in nuts, seeds, and vegetable oils.

- **Minerals:**
    - **Calcium:** Vital for bone and teeth development. Dairy products, fortified plant-based milks, and leafy greens are rich in calcium.
    - **Iron:** Essential for the formation of red blood cells and oxygen transport. Iron-rich foods include red meat, beans, lentils, and fortified cereals.
    - **Zinc:** Supports immune function, wound healing, and growth. Good sources include meat, shellfish, legumes, and seeds.
    - **Iodine:** Important for thyroid function and cognitive development. Iodized salt, dairy products, and seafood are primary sources.
    - **Magnesium:** Necessary for muscle function, nerve transmission, and energy production. It is found in nuts, seeds, whole grains, and leafy greens.

Hydration: Adequate hydration is essential for children as it supports various bodily functions, including temperature regulation, digestion, and cognitive performance. Water should be the primary beverage, with limited consumption of sugary drinks. Encourage children to drink water regularly throughout the day, especially during physical activity.

Balanced Diet:

A balanced diet that includes a variety of foods from all food groups ensures that children receive all the essential nutrients they need for optimal growth and development. Emphasise the importance of consuming a rainbow of fruits and vegetables, whole grains, lean proteins, and healthy fats.

Meal Planning and Healthy Recipes

Creating a well-balanced meal plan for children is key to ensuring they receive the nutrients necessary for healthy growth and development. Meal planning can also help establish healthy eating habits that last a lifetime.

Principles of Meal Planning:

- **Balance:** Ensure each meal contains a balance of carbohydrates, proteins, and fats. Incorporate a variety of food groups to provide a wide range of nutrients.
- **Portion Control:** Serve appropriate portion sizes based on the child's age, activity level, and nutritional needs. Avoid oversized portions to prevent overeating.
- **Variety:** Introduce different foods regularly to prevent mealtime boredom and expose children to various flavours and textures. A diverse diet also helps meet nutritional needs.
- **Colourful Plates:** Encourage meals with colourful fruits and vegetables, which are rich in vitamins, minerals, and antioxidants. A colourful plate is often more appealing to children.

Sample Meal Plans:

- **Breakfast:**
    - **Option 1:** Oatmeal with sliced bananas, a handful of nuts, and a drizzle of honey. Serve with a glass of milk or a dairy alternative.
    - **Option 2:** Whole-grain toast with avocado spread, a boiled egg, and a side of fresh fruit.
    - **Option 3:** Yogurt parfait with mixed berries, granola, and a spoonful of chia seeds.
- **Lunch:**
    - **Option 1:** Turkey and cheese sandwich on whole-grain bread, carrot sticks, and apple slices.
    - **Option 2:** Quinoa salad with grilled chicken, cherry tomatoes, cucumbers, and a lemon vinaigrette.
    - **Option 3:** Veggie wrap with hummus, bell peppers, spinach, and shredded carrots.

- **Dinner:**
  - **Option 1:** Grilled salmon with brown rice, steamed broccoli, and a side salad.
  - **Option 2:** Whole-wheat pasta with marinara sauce, lean ground turkey, and sautéed spinach.
  - **Option 3:** Stir-fried tofu with mixed vegetables and quinoa or brown rice.
- **Snacks:**
  - **Option 1:** Sliced apples with almond butter.
  - **Option 2:** Carrot and cucumber sticks with hummus.
  - **Option 3:** A small bowl of mixed nuts and dried fruit.

Healthy Recipes:

- **Recipe 1: Veggie-Packed Omelet**
  - **Ingredients:** 2 eggs, spinach, bell peppers, onions, tomatoes, and a sprinkle of cheese.
  - **Instructions:** Whisk the eggs in a bowl. Sauté the vegetables in a pan until soft, then pour the eggs over the vegetables. Cook until the eggs are set, and fold the omelet. Serve with whole-grain toast.
- **Recipe 2: Baked Chicken Tenders**
  - **Ingredients:** Chicken breasts, whole-wheat breadcrumbs, grated Parmesan cheese, and olive oil.
  - **Instructions:** Preheat the oven to 400°F (200°C). Cut the chicken into strips. Mix breadcrumbs and Parmesan cheese in a bowl. Dip the chicken strips in olive oil, then coat them with the breadcrumb mixture. Place on a baking sheet and bake for 20-25 minutes until golden brown.
- **Recipe 3: Fruit and Yogurt Smoothie**

- **Ingredients:** 1 cup of yogurt, 1 banana, a handful of berries, and a tablespoon of honey.
- **Instructions:** Combine all ingredients in a blender and blend until smooth. Serve immediately.

- **Recipe 4: Whole-Grain Veggie Pizza**

  - **Ingredients:** Whole-grain pizza dough, tomato sauce, mozzarella cheese, bell peppers, mushrooms, onions, and spinach.
  - **Instructions:** Preheat the oven to 425°F (220°C). Roll out the pizza dough and spread the tomato sauce evenly. Top with cheese and vegetables. Bake for 15-20 minutes until the crust is golden and the cheese is melted.

Breastfeeding vs. Formula Feeding

Feeding an infant is one of the most important decisions a mother will make. Understanding the benefits and considerations of both breastfeeding and formula feeding can help mothers make informed choices that best suit their circumstances.

Benefits of Breastfeeding:

- **Nutritional Superiority:** Breast milk is the optimal source of nutrition for infants. It contains the perfect balance of nutrients, including proteins, fats, vitamins, and antibodies, tailored to the baby's needs. The composition of breast milk changes over time to meet the evolving nutritional requirements of the growing infant.
- **Immune Support:** Breast milk contains antibodies and other immune-boosting elements that protect infants from infections and illnesses. Babies who are breastfed have a lower risk of respiratory infections, ear infections, gastrointestinal issues, and certain chronic conditions like asthma and allergies.
- **Bonding and Emotional Benefits:** Breastfeeding fosters a unique bond between mother and baby. The close physical contact during breastfeeding promotes skin-to-skin interaction, which is soothing for the baby and enhances emotional bonding.
- **Health Benefits for Mothers:** Breastfeeding offers health benefits for mothers as well, including a reduced risk of postpartum depression, faster postpartum recovery, and a lower risk of breast and ovarian cancers.

Challenges of Breastfeeding:

- **Physical Discomfort:** Some mothers experience discomfort, pain, or issues like engorgement, cracked nipples, or mastitis during breastfeeding.
- **Time-Consuming:** Breastfeeding can be time-consuming, particularly for mothers who are balancing work or other responsibilities.
- **Dietary Restrictions:** Mothers who breastfeed may need to monitor their diet closely, as certain foods can affect the baby, and they need to maintain a nutrient-rich diet for their own health.

Formula Feeding:

- **Nutritional Composition:** Infant formula is designed to be a substitute for breast milk, providing essential nutrients to support growth and development. Modern formulas are carefully regulated to ensure they contain adequate amounts of proteins, fats, vitamins, and minerals. Some formulas are fortified with additional nutrients like iron or omega-3 fatty acids.
- **Convenience and Flexibility:** Formula feeding offers convenience, as it allows other caregivers to feed the baby, giving mothers more flexibility. It also enables mothers to manage their time more effectively, especially if they are returning to work.
- **Predictability:** With formula feeding, mothers can measure the exact amount of milk the baby is consuming, which can be reassuring for some parents.

Considerations for Formula Feeding:

- **Cost:** Formula can be expensive, and the cost can add up over time, especially with specialized formulas.
- **Preparation:** Formula requires proper preparation and sterilization of bottles, which adds to the time and effort required.
- **Lack of Immune Support:** Unlike breast milk, formula does not provide antibodies or immune protection, so formula-fed babies may have a higher risk of infections and illnesses.

Combination Feeding:

Some mothers choose to combine breastfeeding and formula feeding, which can offer the benefits of both methods. This approach can be particularly helpful for mothers who need to return to work or who experience challenges with exclusive breastfeeding. Combination feeding allows mothers to maintain a breastfeeding bond while ensuring their baby receives sufficient nutrition through formula.

Support for Feeding Choices:

It is essential for mothers to receive support regardless of their feeding choice. Whether a mother chooses to breastfeed, formula feed, or combine both, access to accurate information, encouragement, and resources is crucial. Healthcare providers, lactation consultants, and support groups can play a significant role in helping mothers navigate feeding decisions.

Managing Food Allergies and Sensitivities

Food allergies and sensitivities in children can be challenging for parents to manage, but with careful planning and knowledge, it is possible to ensure that affected children receive proper nutrition and stay healthy.

Understanding Food Allergies:

- **Definition:** A food allergy occurs when the immune system mistakenly identifies a harmless food protein as a threat and triggers an allergic reaction. Common allergens include milk, eggs, peanuts, tree nuts, soy, wheat, fish, and shellfish.
- **Symptoms:** Allergic reactions can range from mild to severe, with symptoms including hives, swelling, vomiting, diarrhoea, difficulty breathing, and anaphylaxis, a potentially life-threatening condition. Recognizing the signs of an allergic reaction is crucial for prompt treatment.

Managing Food Allergies:

- **Avoidance:** The primary strategy for managing food allergies is complete avoidance of the allergen. This requires careful reading of food labels, communication with caregivers and schools, and vigilance when dining out.
- **Substitutes:** Finding suitable substitutes for allergenic foods is important to ensure that children with allergies receive balanced nutrition. For example, soy or almond milk can replace cow's milk, and sunflower seed butter can substitute for peanut butter.
- **Emergency Plan:** Parents of children with severe allergies should have an emergency action plan, including the use of an epinephrine auto-injector (EpiPen) in case of anaphylaxis. It is essential that caregivers, teachers, and other adults involved in the child's care are aware of the plan.

Understanding Food Sensitivities and Intolerances:

- **Definition:** Food sensitivities or intolerances, unlike allergies, do not involve the immune system. Instead, they occur when the digestive system has difficulty processing certain foods. Common intolerances include lactose intolerance (inability to digest lactose, a sugar found in milk) and gluten sensitivity.

- **Symptoms:** Symptoms of food sensitivities are typically less severe than allergies and may include bloating, gas, diarrhea, or abdominal pain.

Managing Food Sensitivities:

- **Elimination Diet:** An elimination diet, where the suspected food is removed from the diet and then gradually reintroduced, can help identify food sensitivities. Once identified, the offending food should be avoided or limited.
- **Substitutes and Supplements:** For children with lactose intolerance, lactose-free dairy products or calcium-fortified alternatives are available. For gluten sensitivity, gluten-free grains like rice, quinoa, and corn can be used in place of wheat-based products. Supplements may be necessary to ensure adequate nutrient intake.

Emotional and Social Considerations:

- **Education and Communication:** Educating children about their food allergies or sensitivities is important to empower them to make safe choices. Open communication with teachers, friends, and family members ensures that others are aware of the child's dietary needs.
- **Inclusion:** It is important to ensure that children with food allergies or sensitivities do not feel excluded. This may involve providing safe alternatives during social events, school activities, or parties.

Ongoing Monitoring:

As children grow, their food allergies and sensitivities may change. Regular check-ups with a healthcare provider, including potential re-testing for allergies, can help manage these conditions effectively.

THREE

HEALTH AND WELLNESS

Regular Health Check-ups and Immunizations

Regular health check-ups and immunizations are fundamental components of preventive healthcare for children. These measures ensure that children grow up healthy, with timely interventions to prevent or manage potential health issues.

Importance of Regular Health Check-ups:

- **Monitoring Growth and Development:** Health check-ups allow healthcare providers to monitor a child's physical and developmental progress. During these visits, measurements such as height, weight, and head circumference are taken and compared with growth charts to ensure that the child is developing appropriately for their age.
- **Early Detection of Health Issues:** Routine check-ups help detect health problems early when they are often easier to treat. Early detection of issues such as vision or hearing impairments, developmental delays, or nutritional deficiencies can lead to prompt interventions, improving long-term outcomes.
- **Vaccination Updates:** Health check-ups are also an opportunity to review and update a child's vaccination schedule. Ensuring that vaccinations are up-to-date is crucial for protecting children against preventable diseases.
- **Guidance on Health and Nutrition:** These visits provide an opportunity for parents to discuss any concerns with the healthcare provider, including questions about nutrition, behaviour, sleep, or general well-

being. Guidance and education on these topics can help parents support their child's health more effectively.

Schedule of Health Checkups:

- **New-born to 1 Year:** During the first year of life, check-ups are typically scheduled at birth, 1 month, 2 months, 4 months, 6 months, 9 months, and 12 months. These frequent visits are crucial for monitoring the rapid growth and development that occurs during infancy.
- **Toddler Years (1-3 Years):** After the first year, check-ups are generally scheduled at 15 months, 18 months, and 24 months. During this period, growth slows slightly, but developmental milestones such as walking, talking, and social interaction are closely monitored.
- **Preschool and School Age (3-6 Years):** Annual check-ups are recommended during the preschool years. These visits focus on preparing the child for school, including vision and hearing tests, and discussing social and emotional development.
- **School Age (6-12 Years):** Yearly check-ups continue, with an emphasis on academic performance, physical activity, and social relationships. The healthcare provider may also discuss puberty and changes associated with adolescence.
- **Adolescence (13-18 Years):** During adolescence, annual visits remain important to address physical changes, mental health, and lifestyle choices. Discussions may include topics such as nutrition, exercise, substance use, and sexual health.

Immunizations:

- **Role of Immunizations:** Vaccinations are a key part of preventive healthcare, protecting children from serious diseases such as measles, mumps, rubella, polio, and whooping cough. Immunizations work by stimulating the immune system to recognize and fight specific pathogens, thereby preventing illness.
- **Vaccination Schedule:** The immunization schedule is designed to provide protection when children are most vulnerable to specific diseases. Key vaccines include:

    - **Hepatitis B:** Given at birth, 1-2 months, and 6-18 months.

- **Diphtheria, Tetanus, Pertussis (DTaP):** Administered at 2, 4, 6 months, with boosters at 15-18 months and 4-6 years.
- **Measles, Mumps, Rubella (MMR):** First dose at 12-15 months, with a second dose at 4-6 years.
- **Polio (IPV):** Given at 2, 4, 6-18 months, with a booster at 4-6 years.
- **Varicella (Chickenpox):** First dose at 12-15 months, with a second dose at 4-6 years.
- **Influenza:** Annual vaccination is recommended for children 6 months and older.

- **Vaccine Safety:** Vaccines are thoroughly tested for safety and efficacy before being approved for use. Common side effects are usually mild, such as soreness at the injection site or a low-grade fever. Serious side effects are extremely rare, and the benefits of vaccination far outweigh the risks.

Addressing Vaccine Hesitancy:

Vaccine hesitancy can be a challenge for some parents. It's important to discuss concerns with a healthcare provider, who can provide accurate information about the benefits and safety of vaccines. Trustworthy sources of information and open communication can help alleviate fears and encourage vaccination compliance.

Common Childhood Illnesses and Their Management

Children are susceptible to a variety of common illnesses, particularly as they begin to interact more with other children in settings like day care and school. Understanding these illnesses and how to manage them is crucial for parents.

Respiratory Infections:

- **Common Cold:** The common cold is caused by various viruses, leading to symptoms such as a runny nose, cough, sore throat, and mild fever. Management includes rest, hydration, and over-the-counter medications to relieve symptoms. Antibiotics are not effective against colds since they are viral in nature.
- **Influenza (Flu):** The flu is a more severe respiratory infection caused by the influenza virus, with symptoms including high fever, body aches, fatigue, and cough. Antiviral medications can be prescribed if caught early, and annual flu vaccination is recommended to reduce the risk.
- **Respiratory Syncytial Virus (RSV):** RSV is a common virus that affects the lungs and respiratory tract, particularly in infants and young children. Symptoms include a runny nose, coughing, and wheezing. Severe cases may require hospitalization, especially in very young infants.

Gastrointestinal Issues:

- **Gastroenteritis:** Also known as the stomach flu, gastroenteritis causes vomiting, diarrhoea, and abdominal pain. It is usually viral but can also be caused by bacteria or parasites. Management includes keeping the child hydrated with fluids and electrolytes. In some cases, medical attention is needed if dehydration occurs.
- **Constipation:** Constipation is common in children and can cause discomfort and pain during bowel movements. It's often due to a low-fibre diet, dehydration, or withholding stools. Increasing fibre intake, encouraging regular toilet habits, and ensuring adequate hydration can help manage constipation.
- **Reflux (GERD):** Gastro oesophageal reflux disease (GERD) occurs when stomach acid frequently flows back into the oesophagus, causing discomfort and irritability, especially in infants. Management may include dietary changes, feeding position adjustments, and in some

cases, medication.

Skin Conditions:

- **Eczema (Atopic Dermatitis):** Eczema is a chronic skin condition characterized by dry, itchy, and inflamed skin. Management involves moisturizing the skin, avoiding triggers (like certain soaps or fabrics), and using topical corticosteroids for flare-ups.
- **Diaper Rash:** Diaper rash is a common irritation of the skin caused by prolonged exposure to wet or soiled diapers. Frequent diaper changes, barrier creams, and allowing the skin to air out can help prevent and treat diaper rash.
- **Chickenpox:** Chickenpox is a highly contagious viral infection that causes an itchy rash with red spots and blisters. It is usually mild in children but can cause complications in some cases. The varicella vaccine is effective in preventing chickenpox. If contracted, treatment focuses on relieving symptoms with antihistamines, calamine lotion, and fever reducers.

Childhood Fevers:

- **Understanding Fevers:** Fever is a common symptom in children and is often a sign that the body is fighting an infection. While fevers can be concerning for parents, they are generally not harmful and can be managed at home.
- **When to Seek Medical Attention:** Seek medical care if a child's fever is very high (above 104°F or 40°C), lasts more than three days, or is accompanied by symptoms like difficulty breathing, persistent vomiting, or a rash.
- **Managing Fevers:** To manage a fever, keep the child comfortable, offer plenty of fluids, and use fever-reducing medications like acetaminophen or ibuprofen as directed. Ensure the child is not overdressed, and monitor their temperature regularly.

Ear Infections:

- **Otitis Media:** Otitis media is an infection of the middle ear, common in young children. Symptoms include ear pain, irritability, and sometimes fever. While some ear infections resolve on their own, others may require antibiotics. Pain can be managed with over-the-counter pain relievers.

Understanding and Managing Allergies:

- **Seasonal Allergies:** Also known as hay fever, seasonal allergies are triggered by pollen, dust, or mould, leading to symptoms like sneezing, runny nose, and itchy eyes. Management includes avoiding allergens, using antihistamines, and sometimes prescription medications.
- **Food Allergies:** Food allergies can cause reactions ranging from mild (hives, itching) to severe (anaphylaxis). Management involves avoiding allergenic food and carrying emergency medication like an epinephrine auto-injector (Epicene).

Oral Hygiene and Dental Care

Oral hygiene is a crucial aspect of overall health. Establishing good dental care habits early on can prevent cavities, gum disease, and other oral health issues.

Importance of Oral Hygiene:

- **Preventing Cavities:** Cavities are the most common chronic disease in children. They occur when bacteria in the mouth produce acid that erodes the enamel, leading to tooth decay. Regular brushing and flossing, along with a healthy diet, are key to preventing cavities.
- **Gum Health:** Healthy gums are essential for maintaining overall oral health. Gingivitis, or inflammation of the gums, can lead to more severe gum disease if not treated. Proper brushing and regular dental check-ups can prevent gum problems.
- **Impact on Overall Health:** Poor oral hygiene can affect more than just the mouth. Gum disease has been linked to other health issues, such as heart disease and diabetes, making dental care an important aspect of general health.

Establishing Good Oral Hygiene Habits:

- **Brushing and Flossing:** Children should begin brushing their teeth as soon as the first tooth appears. Use a soft-bristled toothbrush and fluoride toothpaste. Brushing should be done twice a day, and flossing should start when teeth begin to touch. Parents should supervise brushing and flossing until the child is capable of doing it effectively on their own, usually around age 6-7.
- **Fluoride Use:** Fluoride helps strengthen tooth enamel and prevent decay. It is important to use fluoride toothpaste and, in some cases, fluoride supplements if recommended by a dentist. Many communities also add fluoride to tap water, providing additional protection against cavities.
- **Diet and Dental Health:** A balanced diet is important for oral health. Limit sugary snacks and drinks, which can lead to tooth decay. Encourage children to drink water, especially fluoridated tap water, and to eat a variety of fruits and vegetables.

Regular Dental Checkups:

- **First Dental Visit:** The American Academy of Paediatric Dentistry recommends that children visit the dentist by their first birthday or within six months of their first tooth appearing. Early visits help establish a dental home and allow the dentist to monitor the child's oral development.
- **Frequency of Visits:** Regular dental check-ups, usually every six months, are important for maintaining oral health. During these visits, the dentist will clean the child's teeth, check for cavities, and provide guidance on proper oral care at home.
- **Sealants and Protective Measures:** Dental sealants are thin coatings applied to the chewing surfaces of the back teeth (molars) to prevent cavities. They are especially beneficial for children as their molars are more prone to decay. The dentist may also recommend fluoride treatments to further protect the teeth.

Managing Dental Issues:

- **Cavities and Fillings:** If a cavity is detected, the dentist will remove the decayed portion of the tooth and fill it with a dental material. Early treatment of cavities prevents more serious dental problems.
- **Orthodontic Concerns:** As children grow, they may develop alignment issues with their teeth or jaws. Early orthodontic evaluations, typically around age 7, can help identify problems that may require braces or other corrective measures.
- **Injury Prevention:** Children are prone to dental injuries, especially during sports or active play. Mouth-guards can help protect the teeth from injury. If a tooth is knocked out or damaged, immediate dental care is essential.

Sleep Patterns and Tips for Better Sleep

Adequate sleep is vital for a child's physical and mental development. Establishing healthy sleep patterns and creating a conducive sleep environment can significantly impact a child's overall well-being.

Importance of Sleep for Children:

- **Physical Growth:** Sleep plays a critical role in physical growth and development. Growth hormone, which stimulates growth and cell reproduction, is primarily released during deep sleep.
- **Cognitive Development:** Sleep is essential for cognitive functions such as memory, learning, and problem-solving. Children who get enough sleep are more alert, attentive, and able to perform better academically.
- **Emotional Well-being:** Lack of sleep can lead to mood swings, irritability, and behavioural issues. Adequate sleep helps regulate emotions and improves overall mood and behaviour.

Recommended Sleep Durations:

- **Infants (0-12 Months):** New-borns typically need 14-17 hours of sleep in a 24-hour period, including naps. As they grow, the total sleep duration gradually decreases to about 12-15 hours by 12 months.
- **Toddlers (1-3 Years):** Toddlers need about 11-14 hours of sleep per day, including naps. Establishing a consistent bedtime routine is important during this stage.
- **Pre-schoolers (3-5 Years):** Pre-schoolers require 10-13 hours of sleep. While naps may decrease or stop during this period, a consistent bedtime routine remains crucial.
- **School-age Children (6-12 Years):** Children in this age group need 9-12 hours of sleep per night. As they become more involved in school and extracurricular activities, maintaining a regular sleep schedule becomes important.
- **Adolescents (13-18 Years):** Adolescents require 8-10 hours of sleep, but many do not get enough due to academic pressures and social activities. Encouraging good sleep habits is essential for their health and academic success.

Tips for Better Sleep:

- **Establish a Bedtime Routine:** A consistent bedtime routine helps signal to the child that it's time to wind down and prepare for sleep. Activities like reading, taking a bath, or listening to calming music can be part of this routine.
- **Create a Sleep-Friendly Environment:** The bedroom should be quiet, dark, and cool, creating an ideal environment for sleep. A comfortable mattress and pillows, along with minimal distractions like electronic devices, can help promote better sleep.
- **Limit Screen Time:** Exposure to screens (TV, tablets, phones) before bed can interfere with the ability to fall asleep. It's best to turn off screens at least an hour before bedtime to allow the child to unwind.
- **Encourage Physical Activity:** Regular physical activity during the day can help children fall asleep faster and enjoy deeper sleep. However, avoid vigorous exercise close to bedtime.
- **Set a Consistent Sleep Schedule:** Going to bed and waking up at the same time each day, even on weekends, helps regulate the child's internal clock and improves sleep quality.
- **Manage Stress and Anxiety:** Children can experience stress and anxiety, which can affect their sleep. Encouraging open communication, practising relaxation techniques, and ensuring a supportive home environment can help alleviate these issues.

Addressing Sleep Issues:

- **Night Waking:** It's common for children, especially infants and toddlers, to wake up during the night. Responding calmly and consistently to night waking can help them learn to soothe themselves back to sleep.
- **Nightmares and Night Terrors:** Nightmares are common in children and usually occur during the second half of the night. Comforting the child and discussing the nightmare can help ease their fears. Night terrors, on the other hand, occur during deep sleep and may require a different approach, such as ensuring the child's safety and gently guiding them back to sleep.
- **Sleep Apnea:** Some children may have sleep apnea, a condition where breathing stops and starts during sleep. Symptoms include loud snoring, gasping, or pauses in breathing. If sleep apnoea is suspected, a healthcare

provider should be consulted for further evaluation and treatment.

FOUR
PHYSICAL DEVELOPMENT

Milestones in Physical Development

Physical development in children involves the growth and refinement of motor skills, from infancy through adolescence. Understanding these milestones helps parents track their child's progress and identify any potential delays early on.

Infancy (0-12 Months):

- **Gross Motor Skills:** These involve large muscle movements. During the first few months, infants begin to gain control over their heads, followed by the ability to roll over (around 4-6 months). By 7-9 months, many babies start to sit independently and may begin to crawl. By their first birthday, many infants are pulling themselves up to stand and may start taking their first steps.
- **Fine Motor Skills:** These involve smaller movements such as grasping. Newborns initially have a reflexive grasp but gradually gain voluntary control. By 4-5 months, infants can reach out and grab objects. By 9-12 months, they develop the pincer grasp, allowing them to pick up small objects with their thumb and forefinger.

Toddler Years (1-3 Years):

- **Walking and Running:** Most toddlers start walking independently by 12-15 months. By 18-24 months, they begin running, although their gait may be unsteady at first. By 3 years, they can run more smoothly and start to engage in activities like climbing and jumping.

- **Coordination and Balance:** As toddlers develop, their coordination and balance improve. By 2 years, many can walk up and down stairs with assistance, and by 3 years, they can pedal a tricycle, kick a ball, and begin to throw and catch objects with more accuracy.
- **Fine Motor Skills:** During this stage, toddlers improve their ability to manipulate small objects. By 2 years, they can build simple block towers, use utensils, and start drawing basic shapes. By 3 years, they begin to show a preference for one hand, often referred to as hand dominance.

Pre-school Years (3-5 Years):

- **Advanced Motor Skills:** By 4-5 years, children can perform more complex physical activities, such as hopping on one foot, skipping, and beginning to ride a bicycle with training wheels. Their running becomes more coordinated, and they can catch a ball more reliably.
- **Fine Motor Skills:** Pre-schoolers refine their ability to use their hands and fingers. They can draw simple pictures, cut with scissors, and dress themselves with minimal assistance. By age 5, many children can write some letters and numbers.

School-Age Years (6-12 Years):

- **Skill Refinement:** As children grow, their motor skills become more refined and coordinated. They can engage in a wide range of physical activities, such as playing sports, dancing, and swimming. Their stamina and strength increase, allowing for longer periods of activity.
- **Fine Motor Skills:** School-age children continue to improve their writing, drawing, and craft skills. By 8-10 years, they can write neatly, tie shoelaces, and perform tasks that require precision, such as building models or playing musical instruments.

Adolescence (13-18 Years):

- **Physical Maturation:** Adolescents experience significant physical changes due to puberty, including growth spurts, the development of secondary sexual characteristics, and increased muscle mass. These changes can vary widely in timing and pace among individuals.

- **Strength and Endurance:** During adolescence, physical strength and endurance increase, allowing teens to participate in more demanding physical activities, including competitive sports.
- **Fine Motor Skills:** While fine motor skills are largely developed by this stage, adolescents continue to refine them, particularly in activities that require precision, such as art, playing instruments, or using tools.

Identifying Delays:

Parents should be aware of typical developmental milestones, but it's also important to recognize that children develop at their own pace. However, significant delays in reaching milestones, such as not walking by 18 months or not speaking by 2 years, may warrant further evaluation by a healthcare professional. Early intervention can be crucial in addressing developmental issues.

Encouraging Physical Activity

Physical activity is vital for children's health, contributing to their physical, mental, and emotional development. Encouraging regular activity helps establish lifelong habits that promote overall well-being.

Benefits of Physical Activity:

- **Physical Health:** Regular physical activity strengthens muscles and bones, improves cardiovascular health, and helps maintain a healthy weight. It also enhances coordination, balance, and flexibility, reducing the risk of injuries.
- **Mental Health:** Exercise releases endorphins, which can improve mood and reduce symptoms of anxiety and depression. Physical activity also enhances cognitive function, improving focus, memory, and academic performance.
- **Social Skills:** Participating in group activities, such as team sports or playground games, helps children develop social skills, including teamwork, cooperation, and communication. It also provides opportunities to make friends and build relationships.
- **Building Confidence:** Mastering physical skills, whether it's learning to ride a bike or scoring a goal, boosts self-esteem and confidence. Children who are active often feel more capable and are more willing to try new challenges.

Age-Appropriate Activities:

- **Infants:** Tummy time is crucial for infants as it helps develop neck and shoulder muscles and prepares them for crawling. Encouraging movement through play, such as reaching for toys or rolling, supports early motor development.
- **Toddlers:** Toddlers should be encouraged to explore their environment through activities like walking, running, climbing, and playing with balls. Structured activities, such as music and movement classes, can also be beneficial.
- **Pre-Schoolers:** At this age, children enjoy activities that involve both gross and fine motor skills, such as riding tricycles, dancing, playing catch, and drawing. Playgrounds offer opportunities for climbing, sliding, and swinging, which are great for physical development.

- **School-Age Children:** Encourage participation in organized sports, dance, martial arts, or other activities that interest them. School-age children should engage in at least 60 minutes of moderate to vigorous physical activity each day.
- **Adolescents:** Adolescents should continue to engage in regular physical activity, including sports, gym workouts, or outdoor activities like hiking or cycling. Encouraging them to stay active can help manage stress and maintain physical health during these crucial developmental years.

Creating a Supportive Environment:

- **Positive Reinforcement:** Praise and encouragement are key to fostering a love of physical activity. Celebrate achievements, no matter how small, to build confidence and motivation.
- **Family Involvement:** Families that are active together are more likely to raise children who value physical fitness. Plan regular family outings that include physical activities, such as biking, hiking, or playing sports together.
- **Limit Screen Time:** Reducing screen time encourages children to be more physically active. Set limits on the time spent on electronic devices and encourage outdoor play or participation in sports instead.

Safe Play Environments

Creating safe play environments is essential to prevent injuries and ensure that children can enjoy their physical activities without unnecessary risks.

Importance of Safety in Play:

- **Preventing Injuries:** Accidental injuries are a leading cause of emergency room visits for children. Ensuring that play areas are safe can significantly reduce the risk of falls, cuts, and other injuries.
- **Promoting Confidence:** When children feel safe, they are more likely to engage fully in play, explore their surroundings, and develop their physical and social skills. A safe environment encourages active participation and reduces fear or anxiety.
- **Supporting Development:** Safe play environments provide opportunities for children to challenge themselves physically and mentally, promoting healthy development. When risks are managed appropriately, children can explore and learn from their experiences.

Creating Safe Indoor Play Spaces:

- **Home Safety:** Ensure that indoor play areas are free from hazards such as sharp edges, electrical outlets, and heavy furniture that can tip over. Use safety gates to block off stairs and secure windows to prevent falls.
- **Toy Safety:** Choose age-appropriate toys that are free from small parts that could be choking hazards. Regularly inspect toys for wear and tear, and discard any that are broken or unsafe.
- **Supervision:** Always supervise young children during play, especially when they are using equipment like swings, slides, or trampolines. Even in a safe environment, accidents can happen, so keeping a close watch is crucial.

Creating Safe Outdoor Play Spaces:

- **Playground Safety:** When visiting playgrounds, check that equipment is well-maintained and that surfaces underneath are soft, such as sand, wood chips, or rubber mats, to cushion falls. Ensure that the playground is age-appropriate for your child.

- **Backyard Safety:** If you have a backyard play area, make sure it is fenced and free from hazards like sharp tools, toxic plants, or exposed electrical wiring. Regularly check equipment like swings or climbing frames for stability and safety.
- **Water Safety:** If there is a pool, ensure that it is fenced with a self-closing, self-latching gate. Never leave children unattended near water, even for a moment. Teach children about water safety and the importance of following rules around pools, lakes, or beaches.

Safety Gear and Equipment:

- **Helmets and Pads:** When riding bikes, scooters, or skateboards, children should always wear helmets, and in some cases, knee and elbow pads. Proper safety gear can prevent serious injuries in the event of a fall or collision.
- **Seat Belts and Car Seats:** Ensure that children are in the appropriate car seat or booster seat for their age, height, and weight. Always use seat belts, even for short trips, to keep children safe in the car.
- **Sports Safety:** For organized sports, make sure children wear the appropriate protective gear, such as mouthguards, shin guards, or goggles. Follow guidelines for safe play, including proper warm-up and cool-down routines.

Importance of Outdoor Activities

Outdoor activities are crucial for children's physical and mental development. Spending time outdoors promotes a healthy lifestyle and offers unique opportunities for growth and learning.

Benefits of Outdoor Activities:

- **Physical Health:** Outdoor activities encourage physical movement, which strengthens muscles, improves cardiovascular health, and helps maintain a healthy weight. Activities like running, climbing, and jumping are excellent for developing gross motor skills.
- **Mental Health:** Being in nature reduces stress, anxiety, and symptoms of attention deficit disorders. Outdoor play fosters creativity, problem-solving, and cognitive development as children engage with their environment.
- **Social Development:** Outdoor settings provide opportunities for social interaction with peers, fostering teamwork, communication, and cooperation. Playing in groups helps children develop important social skills and build friendships.
- **Connection to Nature:** Spending time outdoors helps children develop an appreciation for nature and the environment. This connection can foster a lifelong respect for the natural world and encourage environmentally responsible behaviours.

Encouraging Outdoor Play:

- **Daily Routine:** Incorporate outdoor play into the daily routine, whether it's a walk to the park, a game of tag in the backyard, or a nature hike on weekends. Consistent exposure to outdoor environments helps children see outdoor activities as a normal part of life.
- **Variety of Activities:** Offer a variety of outdoor activities to keep children engaged. This can include traditional sports, nature exploration, gardening, or creative play like building forts or obstacle courses.
- **Unstructured Play:** Allow time for unstructured outdoor play, where children can use their imagination and creativity. Unstructured play is crucial for developing problem-solving skills and independent thinking.

- **Seasonal Activities:** Take advantage of seasonal changes to introduce new outdoor experiences. For example, in the summer, children can enjoy swimming, biking, or camping. In the winter, they can engage in activities like sledging, ice skating, or building snowmen.

Overcoming Barriers to Outdoor Play:

- **Weather Considerations:** While extreme weather can be a barrier, children can still enjoy outdoor play in most conditions with appropriate clothing and gear. Encourage outdoor activities in all seasons to build resilience and adaptability.
- **Safety Concerns:** Address safety concerns by choosing appropriate outdoor locations and supervising play as needed. Educate children about outdoor safety, such as staying within sight, avoiding dangerous areas, and being aware of their surroundings.
- **Screen Time:** Limit screen time to encourage more outdoor play. Setting clear boundaries on the use of electronic devices can motivate children to spend more time being active outdoors.

Involving the Community:

- **Community Resources:** Take advantage of community resources such as parks, playgrounds, and nature centres. Many communities offer organized outdoor activities and events that provide safe and structured opportunities for children to be active.
- **School Involvement:** Advocate for outdoor play and physical education in schools. Schools that prioritize outdoor activities and recess time contribute to the overall well-being of their students.
- **Family Participation:** Make outdoor activities a family affair. When parents and siblings participate, children are more likely to enjoy and look forward to spending time outside.

FIVE
EMOTIONAL AND SOCIAL DEVELOPMENT

Understanding and Managing Emotions

Emotional development is at the heart of early childhood, laying the groundwork for a child's ability to navigate social relationships and face life's challenges. During the early years, children learn to recognize, express, and regulate their emotions—a process that is crucial for their long-term mental and emotional well-being.

Recognizing and Naming Emotions:

Children first need to understand what emotions are and how to identify them. As a mother, you can start by teaching your child to recognize basic emotions such as happiness, sadness, anger, and fear. Use picture books, facial expression games, and everyday situations to introduce these concepts. For instance, when your child is frustrated, you might say, "It looks like you're feeling angry because your block tower fell over." This not only helps them label their feelings but also validates their emotional experiences.

Emotional Expression and Communication:

Encouraging children to express their emotions is vital. When children feel safe to express how they feel, they are less likely to internalize stress or act out in negative ways. Encourage open communication by listening actively to your child, showing empathy, and asking open-ended questions like, "How did that make you feel?" or "What can we do to make you feel better?" This practice not only strengthens your bond but also teaches your child that their feelings matter and can be communicated effectively.

Developing Coping Mechanisms:

As children grow, they need to learn how to manage their emotions, especially in challenging situations. Teach your child simple coping strategies, such as deep breathing, counting to ten, or taking a break in a calm space. These techniques can be practised regularly, so they become second nature when your child is upset or overwhelmed. You might also role-play different scenarios to help your child understand how to handle various emotional situations, such as dealing with disappointment or anger.

Parental Role in Emotional Modelling:

Children often mirror the emotional responses of their caregivers. By managing your emotions in a healthy way, you set a positive example for your child. For instance, if you're feeling stressed, instead of reacting impulsively, you might take a deep breath and calmly explain, "I'm feeling a bit overwhelmed right now, so I'm going to take a minute to relax." This teaches your child that it's okay to have strong emotions, but it's also important to handle them thoughtfully.

Building Empathy:

Empathy is the ability to understand and share the feelings of others, and it's a crucial component of emotional intelligence. Encourage your child to think about how others might be feeling in different situations. For example, if a friend is upset, you can ask your child, "How do you think they're feeling right now?" and "What could you do to help them feel better?" Developing empathy helps children build strong, supportive relationships and fosters kindness and consideration for others.

Building Social Skills and Friendships

Social skills are essential for a child's ability to form meaningful relationships and interact successfully with others. These skills, developed during early childhood, lay the foundation for healthy friendships and social interactions throughout life.

Developing Communication Skills:

Communication is a key component of social interactions. Teach your child the importance of listening when others speak, using polite language, and expressing themselves clearly. Role-playing can be a useful tool in helping your child practice conversations, such as how to introduce themselves, ask for something, or resolve a disagreement. Reinforce positive communication by praising your child when they use these skills effectively.

Understanding Social Norms and Cues:

Children need to learn social norms, such as taking turns, sharing, and respecting personal space. These concepts can be taught through games, group activities, and structured playdates. Additionally, help your child recognize social cues, such as body language and facial expressions, which are critical for understanding others' feelings and intentions. You can play guessing games where you mimic different emotions and ask your child to identify them, helping them become more attuned to these non-verbal signals.

Fostering Friendships:

Friendship is a vital aspect of social development. Encourage your child to be friendly, inclusive, and considerate towards others. Teach them the importance of qualities like honesty, kindness, and trust in maintaining friendships. You can also guide them on how to navigate conflicts with friends, emphasizing the importance of communication and compromise. Support your child's efforts to make and maintain friendships by arranging playdates, encouraging group activities, and providing opportunities for social interaction in various settings.

Encouraging Positive Behaviour

Fostering positive behaviour in children not only creates a harmonious home environment but also helps children develop self-discipline, respect, and responsibility. Positive behaviour stems from clear expectations, consistent guidance, and supportive reinforcement.

Setting Clear Expectations and Boundaries:

Children thrive when they understand what is expected of them. Establishing clear, consistent rules helps children learn boundaries and understand the consequences of their actions. When setting rules, explain them in a way your child can understand and connect them to values like respect, safety, and kindness. For instance, you might say, "We don't hit because it hurts others, and we want to keep everyone safe." Reinforce these rules consistently, and be sure to model the behaviour you wish to see in your child.

Positive Reinforcement and Praise:

Positive reinforcement is one of the most effective ways to encourage desirable behaviour. Praise your child when they demonstrate good behaviour, such as sharing, being polite, or completing a task without being asked. Be specific in your praise, saying things like, "I really appreciate how you cleaned up your toys without being reminded." This not only reinforces the behaviour but also boosts your child's self-esteem and motivation to continue behaving well.

Building Responsibility and Independence:

Encouraging your child to take responsibility for their actions helps them develop a sense of independence and accountability. Assign age-appropriate chores and responsibilities, such as tidying their room, feeding a pet, or helping set the table. Offer guidance and support, but allow them to complete tasks on their own. Celebrate their efforts and accomplishments, even if the results aren't perfect. This approach fosters a sense of pride and ownership, which is essential for developing self-discipline and a strong work ethic.

Using Logical Consequences:

When addressing negative behaviour, it's important to use logical consequences that are directly related to the behaviour. For example, if your child refuses to put away their toys, a logical consequence might be that they can't play with those toys until they are put away. This approach helps children understand the connection between their actions and the outcomes, promoting better decision-making in the future.

Creating a Positive and Supportive Environment:

A positive home environment is crucial for encouraging good behaviour. Create a space where your child feels safe, valued, and supported. Provide opportunities for your child to succeed and grow by setting up routines, offering choices, and allowing for exploration and creativity. Ensure that your child knows they are loved and appreciated, regardless of their behaviour, as this unconditional support forms the foundation of their confidence and well-being.

Consistency in Discipline:

Consistency is the key to effective discipline. Make sure that rules and consequences are applied consistently across situations and caregivers. Inconsistent discipline can confuse children and undermine the lessons you are trying to teach. If both parents or caregivers are involved, it's important that they are on the same page regarding expectations and consequences, providing a united front that helps the child feel secure and understand the boundaries.

Handling Tantrums and Discipline Strategies

Tantrums are a normal part of early childhood as children learn to navigate their emotions and test boundaries. Handling tantrums effectively and employing thoughtful discipline strategies can help children develop better emotional regulation and behaviour over time.

Understanding the Roots of Tantrums:

Tantrums typically arise from frustration, overstimulation, or unmet needs. Recognizing the underlying causes of tantrums, such as hunger, fatigue, or the inability to express emotions verbally, can help you address the problem before it escalates. It's important to remember that tantrums are a normal part of development, especially in toddlers who are learning to assert their independence.

Preventing Tantrums:

Preventing tantrums is often more effective than dealing with them once they've started. Establish a consistent daily routine that includes regular meals, naps, and playtime. Offer choices to give your child a sense of control, such as selecting their clothes or choosing between two snacks. Ensure that your child gets plenty of physical activity and opportunities for independent play, which can reduce frustration and pent-up energy.

Managing Tantrums When They Occur:

When a tantrum happens, the key is to stay calm and composed. Reacting with anger or frustration can exacerbate the situation. Instead, acknowledge your child's feelings and offer comfort if they are receptive. You might say, "I see you're very upset because you wanted to keep playing, but it's time to go." If possible, redirect their attention to something else, or if they need space, allow them a safe area to calm down.

Consistent Discipline Strategies:

Discipline during or after a tantrum should be consistent and fair. For example, if a tantrum was triggered by not getting a toy, explain calmly why the toy was not given and enforce any related consequences, such as a time-out or losing the privilege to play with that toy for a certain period. Ensure that the consequences are related to the behavior and are applied consistently, so your child learns from the experience.

Post-Tantrum Discussions:

After a tantrum has subsided, it's important to talk to your child about what happened. Discuss the emotions they were feeling, and why the tantrum occurred, and explore better ways to handle similar situations in the future. This conversation reinforces emotional awareness and provides an opportunity for learning and growth. Reassure your child that they are loved, and emphasize that while the behaviour was not acceptable, they are always supported.

SIX

COGNITIVE DEVELOPMENT

Stimulating Cognitive Growth Through Play

Play is not just a leisure activity for children; it is a powerful tool for cognitive development. Through play, children explore their environment, develop problem-solving skills, and learn about cause and effect. As a mother, you can use playtime to nurture your child's cognitive abilities and encourage lifelong learning.

The Role of Play in Cognitive Development:

Play allows children to engage with their surroundings in a meaningful way, fostering critical thinking and creativity. During play, children often encounter challenges that require them to think critically, make decisions, and solve problems. For example, building a tower with blocks involves understanding balance and gravity, while imaginative play helps children explore different scenarios and outcomes. These experiences are essential for developing cognitive skills such as memory, attention, and reasoning.

Types of Play and Their Cognitive Benefits:

Different types of play contribute to cognitive development in various ways. Constructive play, like building with blocks or drawing, enhances spatial awareness, fine motor skills, and problem-solving abilities. Pretend play or role-playing allows children to experiment with different roles and scenarios, fostering creativity, language skills, and social understanding. Physical play supports cognitive development by improving coordination and understanding of spatial concepts.

Incorporating Learning into Play:

To maximize the cognitive benefits of play, incorporate learning opportunities into everyday activities. Simple games like sorting shapes, counting objects, or identifying colours can enhance cognitive skills. For example, when playing with building blocks, ask your child to count the blocks, identify their colours, or sort them by size. These activities reinforce concepts like numbers, colours, and patterns in a fun and engaging way.

The Importance of Open-Ended Play:

Open-ended play, where there is no specific goal or outcome, encourages creativity and independent thinking. Provide your child with toys that can be used in multiple ways, such as blocks, art supplies, or playdough. These types of toys allow children to explore, experiment, and use their imagination, leading to deeper cognitive engagement.

Parental Involvement in Play:

While independent play is important, parental involvement can enhance the cognitive benefits of play. Join your child in their play activities, offer gentle guidance, and introduce new concepts or challenges. For example, if your child is playing with a toy kitchen, you might introduce the concept of measurements or ask them to create a menu. Your involvement not only enriches the play experience but also strengthens your bond with your child.

Encouraging Play Across Different Domains:

Encourage your child to engage in a variety of play activities that stimulate different cognitive domains. For instance, puzzles and board games can improve logical thinking and strategy, while outdoor play can enhance observational skills and understanding of nature. By providing diverse play experiences, you help your child develop a well-rounded set of cognitive skills.

Reading and Storytelling

Reading and storytelling are vital tools in cognitive development, fostering language skills, imagination, and a love for learning. These activities not only support cognitive growth but also strengthen the emotional bond between mother and child.

The Cognitive Benefits of Reading:

Reading to your child from an early age exposes them to new vocabulary, sentence structures, and concepts, which are essential for language development. As you read, your child learns to recognize words, understand their meanings, and make connections between spoken and written language. This early exposure to reading also enhances memory and concentration, as children learn to follow the narrative and anticipate what comes next.

Storytelling as a Cognitive Tool:

Storytelling engages your child's imagination, encouraging them to think creatively and critically. When you tell a story, your child is prompted to visualize characters, settings, and events, which enhances their ability to think abstractly. Moreover, storytelling helps children understand cause-and-effect relationships, sequence of events, and moral lessons, all of which are important cognitive skills.

Interactive Reading and Storytelling:

Make reading and storytelling interactive to deepen cognitive engagement. Ask your child questions about the story, such as, "What do you think will happen next?" or "Why do you think the character did that?" This encourages them to think critically and make predictions. You can also involve them in the storytelling process by asking them to finish a story or create their own endings. This not only enhances their cognitive skills but also boosts their confidence and creativity.

Creating a Reading-Rich Environment:

Surround your child with books and reading materials to encourage a love for reading. Create a cosy reading nook at home with a variety of books that cater to your child's interests and reading level. Regularly introduce new books to keep them engaged and excited about reading. Additionally, set aside dedicated time each day for reading and storytelling, making it a special and enjoyable part of your routine.

The Power of Repetition:

Children often enjoy hearing the same stories repeatedly, which plays an important role in cognitive development. Repetition helps reinforce language patterns, story structure, and vocabulary. Each time a story is read, children may notice new details or make different connections, deepening their understanding and comprehension.

Puzzles and Educational Games

Puzzles and educational games are powerful tools for cognitive development, enhancing skills such as problem-solving, logical thinking, and spatial awareness. These activities are both fun and intellectually stimulating, making them ideal for promoting cognitive growth.

Problem-Solving Through Puzzles:

Puzzles require children to think critically and solve problems by fitting pieces together to form a complete picture. This process involves analyzing shapes, colors, and patterns, and figuring out how they relate to one another. As children work on puzzles, they develop patience, persistence, and the ability to approach problems systematically. Puzzles also enhance hand-eye coordination and fine motor skills as children manipulate the pieces.

Logical Thinking with Educational Games:

Educational games often involve rules, strategies, and goals, which require logical thinking and decision-making. Games like matching cards, memory games, or board games teach children to plan ahead, consider different outcomes, and make informed choices. These skills are fundamental for cognitive development and are transferable to real-life situations, where children need to think logically and solve problems.

Spatial Awareness and Visual Perception:

Puzzles and games that involve matching, sorting, or arranging objects help develop spatial awareness and visual perception. For example, completing a jigsaw puzzle requires understanding how pieces fit together in a space, while sorting games involve recognizing patterns and relationships between objects. These activities enhance a child's ability to visualize and manipulate objects in their mind, which is important for tasks like reading, writing, and navigating their environment.

Cooperative Learning:

Many educational games involve group play, which not only supports cognitive development but also fosters social skills like teamwork, communication, and turn-taking. Playing games with others teaches children how to collaborate, share ideas, and respect rules, which are essential skills for both academic and social success. Cooperative learning through games also provides opportunities for peer learning, where children can learn from each other's strategies and approaches.

Adapting Puzzles and Games to Your Child's Level:

It's important to choose puzzles and games that are appropriate for your child's age and developmental level. Start with simple puzzles and gradually introduce more complex ones as your child's skills improve. The same goes for educational games—begin with basic games and increase the difficulty as your child masters the concepts. This gradual progression helps maintain your child's interest and ensures that they are continually challenged and engaged.

Encouraging Curiosity and Exploration

Curiosity is the driving force behind learning and discovery. By fostering curiosity and encouraging exploration, you help your child develop a lifelong love of learning and a deep understanding of the world around them.

The Importance of Curiosity in Cognitive Development:

Curiosity motivates children to ask questions, seek out new experiences, and explore their environment. This natural desire to learn leads to cognitive growth as children gather information, make connections, and solve problems. Encouraging curiosity helps children become independent thinkers who are not afraid to explore new ideas and concepts.

Creating an Environment for Exploration:

To foster curiosity, create an environment at home that encourages exploration and discovery. Provide your child with access to a variety of materials and resources, such as books, art supplies, building blocks, and nature objects. Set up exploration stations with themed activities, like a science corner with magnifying glasses and specimens, or an art area with different mediums to experiment with. Ensure that your child feels safe to explore and make mistakes, as this is a key part of the learning process.

Encouraging Questions and Critical Thinking:

When your child asks questions, take the time to answer them thoughtfully and encourage further inquiry. For example, if your child asks why the sky is blue, you might explain the basics of light and encourage them to observe the sky at different times of the day. Engage in discussions that prompt critical thinking by asking questions like, “What do you think will happen if we mix these two colours?” or “Why do you think animals hibernate in the winter?” This not only satisfies their curiosity but also deepens their understanding of the world.

Hands-On Learning Experiences:

Hands-on experiences are powerful tools for cognitive development. Encourage your child to learn through doing, whether it’s planting seeds and observing their growth, building structures with blocks, or conducting simple science experiments at home. These activities allow children to explore concepts in a tangible way, reinforcing their learning and sparking further curiosity.

Supporting Your Child’s Interests:

Pay attention to your child’s interests and provide opportunities for them to explore these areas further. If your child shows an interest in dinosaurs, for example, you could visit a museum, read books on the subject, or watch educational videos together. Supporting your child's passions not only fosters curiosity but also builds their confidence and enthusiasm for learning.

Balancing Guidance and Independence:

While it's important to guide your child's exploration, it's equally important to give them the freedom to discover things on their own. Allow your child to explore independently, make choices, and experiment, even if it means making mistakes along the way. This balance of guidance and independence encourages self-directed learning, where your child takes ownership of their education and develops a lifelong love of learning.

SEVEN

EDUCATIONAL DEVELOPMENT

Early Childhood Education Options

Early childhood education (ECE) plays a crucial role in laying the foundation for lifelong learning. Choosing the right early education option for your child is an important decision that can influence their cognitive, social, and emotional development.

Types of Early Childhood Education Programs:

- **Preschool Programs:** Preschools provide a structured environment where children can develop social skills, basic literacy, and numeracy through play-based learning. These programs typically cater to children aged 3 to 5 and emphasize hands-on activities that promote cognitive and motor skills development. Many preschools follow specific educational philosophies, such as Montessori or Reggio Emilia, each with its approach to learning and development.
- **Day-care Centres:** Day-care centres offer childcare services along with early education, catering to children from infancy through preschool age. While the primary focus is on providing a safe and nurturing environment, many day-care centres also incorporate educational activities to support cognitive and social development. This option is particularly suitable for working parents who need full-day care for their children.
- **Home-Based Programs:** Home-based early education programs are provided by licensed caregivers in a home setting. These programs often offer a more personalized approach, with smaller group sizes that allow

for individualized attention. Home-based programs can vary widely in terms of educational content and structure, so it's important to research and select a program that aligns with your educational goals for your child.

- **Head Start Programs:** Head Start is a federally funded program in the United States that provides comprehensive early childhood education, health, nutrition, and parent involvement services to low-income families. These programs are designed to promote school readiness and support the overall development of children from birth to age 5. Head Start programs often include services for children with disabilities and offer support to families to ensure a smooth transition to kindergarten.

Factors to Consider When Choosing an Early Childhood Education Program:

- **Philosophy and Curriculum:** Consider the educational philosophy and curriculum of the program. Some parents may prefer a more academic-focused approach, while others may prioritize play-based or child-led learning environments. It's important to choose a program that aligns with your child's learning style and your family's values.
- **Teacher Qualifications and Experience:** The qualifications and experience of the educators play a significant role in the quality of early childhood education. Look for programs with well-trained, experienced teachers who are knowledgeable about child development and capable of creating a supportive learning environment.
- **Class Size and Teacher-to-Child Ratio:** Smaller class sizes and lower teacher-to-child ratios allow for more individualized attention and a better learning experience. Programs with smaller groups enable teachers to address the unique needs of each child, which is particularly important in the early years when children's development varies widely.
- **Facilities and Resources:** The physical environment of the program should be safe, clean, and conducive to learning. Adequate outdoor play areas, age-appropriate learning materials, and a variety of educational resources are essential for fostering a well-rounded early childhood education.
- **Parental Involvement:** Some early education programs encourage parental involvement through regular communication, volunteer opportunities, and parent-teacher conferences. Consider whether you

want a program that actively involves you in your child's education and development.

Preparing for School

Preparing your child for school is a significant milestone that involves more than just academic readiness. It encompasses social, emotional, and practical skills that will help your child adjust to the school environment and thrive in their educational journey.

Academic Readiness:

- **Basic Literacy and Numeracy:** Before starting school, it's helpful for children to have a basic understanding of letters, numbers, shapes, and colors. You can support this by engaging in activities like reading together, playing counting games, and exploring shapes and patterns through puzzles or drawing. These foundational skills will give your child a head start in the classroom and boost their confidence in learning new concepts.
- **Fine Motor Skills:** Developing fine motor skills is essential for tasks like writing, cutting with scissors, and manipulating small objects. Encourage your child to engage in activities that strengthen these skills, such as coloring, building with blocks, threading beads, or using child-safe scissors. Practicing these skills at home can make the transition to school smoother and more enjoyable.
- **Listening and Following Instructions:** School requires children to listen to instructions, follow rules, and complete tasks independently. You can prepare your child by practicing these skills at home through structured activities, such as cooking together (following a recipe), playing games with rules, or participating in group activities where they need to wait their turn and listen to others.

Social and Emotional Readiness:

- **Separation from Parents:** For many children, starting school marks the first time they will be away from their parents for an extended period. To ease this transition, gradually introduce situations where your child spends time away from you, such as play dates, staying with a relative, or attending a short preschool program. Building trust with other caregivers and feeling secure in new environments will help your child adjust to the school setting.

- **Interacting with Peers:** School is a social environment where children must learn to interact, share, and cooperate with others. Encourage your child to develop social skills by arranging play dates, participating in group activities, and teaching them to resolve conflicts calmly and respectfully. Role-playing different social scenarios can also help your child understand how to navigate friendships and social interactions at school.
- **Emotional Regulation:** Starting school can be overwhelming for young children, and they may experience a range of emotions, from excitement to anxiety. Teach your child strategies for managing their emotions, such as deep breathing, using words to express feelings, or seeking help from a teacher or trusted adult when needed. Discussing what to expect at school and reassuring them that it's normal to feel a mix of emotions can also help ease any fears or anxieties.

Practical Skills for School:

- **Independence in Self-Care:** Encourage your child to practice self-care tasks like dressing themselves, using the restroom independently, and managing their belongings (e.g., putting on their backpack, opening lunch containers). These skills will help them feel more confident and self-reliant at school.
- **Understanding Routines:** Familiarize your child with the concept of routines, as school days often follow a structured schedule. You can create a similar routine at home, with set times for waking up, eating meals, playing, and going to bed. This will help your child adjust to the school day's rhythm and understand the importance of following a schedule.
- **Communication Skills:** Teach your child to communicate their needs, such as asking for help, expressing discomfort, or requesting permission. Practicing these communication skills at home will prepare them to interact effectively with teachers and peers at school.

Visiting the School and Meeting the Teacher:

- **School Visit:** Visiting the school before the first day can help your child feel more comfortable and familiar with the new environment. Walk around the school, show them their classroom, playground, and other important areas, and discuss what they will do during the day. This will help reduce any anxiety about the unknown and build excitement for the new experience.

- **Meeting the Teacher:** If possible, arrange for your child to meet their teacher before school starts. A positive introduction can set the tone for a trusting relationship, making your child feel more at ease in the classroom. Discuss with the teacher any concerns or special needs your child may have, ensuring that their transition to school is as smooth as possible.

Supporting Homework and Study Habits

Developing good homework and study habits is essential for academic success. As a mother, you can create a supportive environment that encourages your child to take responsibility for their learning and develop effective study habits.

Creating a Homework Routine:

- **Establishing a Consistent Schedule:** Set a specific time each day for homework and study. A consistent routine helps your child develop a habit of doing their homework regularly and reduces procrastination. Choose a time that works best for your child, considering their energy levels and after-school activities.
- **Creating a Homework-Friendly Environment:** Designate a quiet, well-lit area in your home where your child can focus on their homework. Ensure that the space is free from distractions, such as television or loud noises, and has all the necessary supplies, like pencils, paper, and a calculator. A comfortable and organized workspace can enhance concentration and productivity.
- **Setting Clear Expectations:** Make it clear that homework is a priority and must be completed before engaging in leisure activities. Set specific goals for each homework session, such as finishing a certain number of math problems or reading a chapter. These goals help your child stay focused and motivated.

Encouraging Independent Work:

- **Fostering Responsibility:** Encourage your child to take responsibility for their homework by keeping track of assignments, understanding instructions, and completing tasks on time. Provide guidance and support when needed, but avoid doing the work for them. This promotes independence and helps your child develop problem-solving skills.
- **Building Time Management Skills:** Teach your child how to manage their time effectively by breaking down larger assignments into smaller, manageable tasks. Use tools like planners, checklists, or timers to help them organize their work and stay on track. Time management is a valuable skill that will benefit your child throughout their academic

journey and beyond.

- **Balancing Homework with Other Activities:** Ensure that your child has a balanced schedule that includes time for homework, extracurricular activities, play, and relaxation. Overloading your child with too many activities can lead to stress and burnout, so it's important to find a balance that allows for both academic and personal growth.

Providing Support and Encouragement:

- **Being Available for Help:** Let your child know that you are available to help if they have questions or need clarification on their homework. Offer guidance by asking questions that lead them to find the answers themselves, rather than providing solutions. This approach encourages critical thinking and reinforces their learning.
- **Praising Effort and Progress:** Recognize and praise your child's effort and progress, rather than focusing solely on the results. Positive reinforcement boosts confidence and motivates your child to keep working hard, even when faced with challenges.
- **Collaborating with Teachers:** Maintain open communication with your child's teachers to stay informed about their progress and any areas where they may need extra support. Collaborating with teachers ensures that your child receives consistent guidance both at school and at home.

Encouraging a Love for Learning

Instilling a love for learning in your child is one of the most valuable gifts you can give them. When children develop a passion for learning, they become curious, motivated, and engaged in their education, setting the stage for lifelong success.

Making Learning Fun and Engaging:

- **Incorporating Play into Learning:** Children learn best when they are having fun. Incorporate play into learning by using educational games, puzzles, and hands-on activities that stimulate curiosity and creativity. Whether it's a science experiment in the kitchen, a nature walk to explore biology, or a math game with cards, integrating play into learning makes it enjoyable and memorable.
- **Encouraging Exploration and Curiosity:** Foster your child's natural curiosity by encouraging them to ask questions, explore new topics, and seek out information. Provide opportunities for discovery, whether through visits to museums, nature trips, or simple experiments at home. Show enthusiasm for their interests and support their exploration by providing resources like books, videos, or materials for projects.
- **Celebrating Achievements:** Celebrate your child's academic achievements, no matter how small. Acknowledging their successes, whether it's mastering a new skill, completing a project, or receiving good grades, reinforces their love for learning and encourages them to strive for further accomplishments.

Modeling a Love for Learning:

- **Being a Role Model:** Children learn by example, so show your enthusiasm for learning by pursuing your own interests and sharing your experiences with your child. Read books, engage in hobbies, or take up new challenges, and let your child see the joy and fulfilment that learning brings.
- **Sharing Learning Experiences:** Engage in learning activities together as a family. Whether it's reading a book, watching an educational documentary, or working on a project, shared learning experiences create positive associations with education and strengthen family bonds.

Supporting Their Interests:

- **Nurturing Passions:** Pay attention to your child's interests and passions, and provide opportunities for them to explore these areas further. Whether it's music, art, science, or sports, supporting your child's passions fosters a love for learning and helps them develop expertise in areas they are passionate about.
- **Allowing for Self-Directed Learning:** Encourage your child to take the lead in their learning by pursuing topics that interest them. Provide resources and guidance, but allow them the freedom to explore at their own pace. Self-directed learning promotes autonomy, critical thinking, and a deeper understanding of subjects that captivate their interest.
- **Encouraging Lifelong Learning:** Emphasize that learning doesn't stop at school. Encourage your child to see learning as a lifelong journey that continues through all stages of life. Instil a mind-set that values curiosity, exploration, and the pursuit of knowledge as essential parts of personal growth and fulfilment.

EIGHT

HABITS AND ROUTINES

Establishing Daily Routines

Daily routines provide structure and stability for children, helping them feel secure and understand what to expect throughout their day. Establishing consistent routines can positively impact their behaviour, development, and overall well-being.

Creating a Structured Routine:

- **Morning Routine:** Start the day with a predictable morning routine that includes essential activities such as waking up, brushing teeth, getting dressed, and having breakfast. A consistent morning routine helps children transition smoothly from sleep to their day's activities and sets a positive tone for the rest of the day.
- **Daily Activities:** Incorporate a sequence of daily activities that include time for play, learning, meals, and rest. For example, allocate specific times for educational activities, free play, and family time. This structure helps children understand the flow of the day and reinforces time management skills.
- **Bedtime Routine:** A calming bedtime routine is crucial for helping children wind down and prepare for sleep. Activities such as reading a story, taking a bath, or listening to soothing music can signal to your child that it's time to relax and get ready for bed. A consistent bedtime routine promotes better sleep patterns and overall health.

Flexibility within Routine:

While routines provide structure, it's also important to allow for some flexibility. Life is unpredictable, and occasional deviations from the routine are inevitable. Teach your child how to adapt to changes while maintaining a sense of stability. For example, if an unexpected event disrupts the routine, calmly explain the situation to your child and adjust the schedule as needed.

Involving Children in Routine Planning:

Involve your child in planning their daily routine to help them feel more engaged and responsible. Allow them to choose certain activities or decide on the order of events within their routine. This involvement fosters a sense of ownership and encourages them to adhere to the routine.

Importance of Consistency

Consistency is key in reinforcing habits and routines, providing children with a sense of security and helping them develop predictable patterns of behaviour.

Building Trust and Security:

Consistent routines help children feel secure and build trust with their caregivers. When children know what to expect, they feel more confident and less anxious. Consistency in routines, such as regular mealtimes and bedtimes, helps create a stable environment where children can thrive emotionally and socially.

Reinforcing Positive Behavior:

Consistency in expectations and consequences is crucial for reinforcing positive behaviour. When rules and guidelines are consistently applied, children learn what is expected of them and understand the consequences of their actions. Consistent discipline helps establish clear boundaries and fosters a sense of responsibility and self-discipline.

Developing Good Habits:

Establishing consistent routines helps children develop good habits, such as regular study times, healthy eating practices, and personal hygiene routines. Repetition and routine reinforce these habits, making them second nature. Over time, these positive habits contribute to a child's overall development and well-being.

Managing Transitions:

Consistency also plays a role in managing transitions, such as starting school or adjusting to new activities. Consistent routines during these transitions provide a familiar structure, helping children adapt more easily to changes. Preparing your child for transitions with a consistent approach can reduce anxiety and make the adjustment period smoother.

Creating a Positive Home Environment

A positive home environment fosters healthy development and contributes to your child's overall happiness and well-being. Creating a nurturing and supportive atmosphere at home involves several key elements.

Emotional Support and Encouragement:

Provide a supportive and loving environment where your child feels valued and respected. Offer encouragement and praise for their efforts, achievements, and positive behaviour. Acknowledge their feelings and provide comfort during difficult times. Emotional support helps build your child's self-esteem and resilience.

Safe and Organized Space:

Create a safe and organized living space where your child can explore, play, and learn. Ensure that the environment is child-proofed and free from potential hazards. An organized space with designated areas for different activities (e.g., play area, study area) helps children understand where and how to engage in various tasks.

Healthy Lifestyle:

Promote a healthy lifestyle by providing nutritious meals, encouraging physical activity, and ensuring adequate sleep. A balanced diet, regular exercise, and proper rest are essential for your child's physical and mental health. Incorporate healthy habits into your family routine, such as family meals and outdoor activities.

Positive Communication:

Foster open and positive communication within the family. Encourage your child to express their thoughts and feelings, and actively listen to what they have to say. Use positive language and offer constructive feedback. Effective communication helps build strong relationships and fosters a sense of belonging and trust.

Family Bonding:

Spend quality time together as a family to strengthen bonds and create lasting memories. Engage in activities that everyone enjoys, such as playing games, cooking together, or going on outings. Family bonding contributes to a supportive and loving home environment where your child feels connected and valued.

Setting Boundaries and Rules:

Establish clear boundaries and rules that are consistent and fair. Ensure that rules are age-appropriate and communicated clearly to your child.

Consistent enforcement of rules helps children understand expectations and fosters a sense of structure and security.

Balancing Screen Time and Other Activities

In today's digital age, managing screen time is crucial for maintaining a balanced lifestyle. Balancing screen time with other activities ensures that children engage in a variety of experiences that support their overall development.

Setting Screen Time Limits:

Establish clear limits on screen time based on your child's age and developmental needs. The American Academy of Paediatrics recommends no more than one hour of screen time per day for children aged 2 to 5 years and consistent limits for older children. Setting limits helps prevent excessive screen time and encourages children to engage in other activities.

Encouraging Active Play:

Promote physical activity by encouraging your child to participate in outdoor play and sports. Active play is essential for physical health, motor skill development, and social interaction. Create opportunities for your child to play outside, join a sports team, or engage in other physical activities that they enjoy.

Fostering Creativity and Imagination:

Support your child's creativity by providing opportunities for imaginative play and creative expression. Encourage activities such as drawing, building with blocks, playing with art supplies, or engaging in role-playing games. Creative activities stimulate cognitive development and allow children to explore their interests and talents.

Promoting Social Interaction:

Facilitate social interaction by organizing play dates, family gatherings, or group activities. Interacting with peers and family members helps children develop social skills, learn to share and cooperate, and build friendships. Social interaction is a key component of emotional and social development.

Modelling Healthy Screen Habits:

Be a role model for healthy screen habits by managing your own screen time and prioritizing face-to-face interactions. Demonstrate balanced use of technology by setting aside time for family activities, engaging in conversation, and participating in offline hobbies. Your behaviour influences your child's screen habits and overall lifestyle.

Creating Screen-Free Zones:

Designate specific areas and times in your home as screen-free zones, such as during mealtimes or before bedtime. This helps create boundaries around screen use and encourages children to focus on other activities. Use these screen-free times to engage in meaningful family interactions or other non-screen-related activities.

Selecting Quality Content:

When screen time is permitted, ensure that the content is educational and age-appropriate. Choose programs, apps, and games that align with your child's developmental stage and interests. High-quality content supports learning and development while keeping screen time engaging and beneficial.

NINE

SEASONAL PROTECTION AND SAFETY

Preparing for Different Seasons

Adapting to the changing seasons requires specific preparations to ensure your child's health and safety. Each season presents unique challenges and opportunities, and being prepared helps keep your child comfortable and protected throughout the year.

Spring and Summer Preparation:

- **Allergy Management:** Spring often brings increased pollen levels, which can trigger allergies in some children. Monitor local pollen forecasts and keep windows closed during high pollen times. Consider using air purifiers and consult with your child's paediatrician about allergy medications or treatments if necessary.
- **Sun Protection:** As temperatures rise and the sun becomes stronger, it's important to protect your child's skin from harmful UV rays. Ensure your child wears sunscreen with a high SPF, protective clothing, and a hat when spending time outdoors. Encourage the use of sunglasses with UV protection to safeguard their eyes.
- **Hydration:** Increased temperatures can lead to dehydration, so encourage your child to drink plenty of water throughout the day. Offer water regularly, especially before, during, and after outdoor activities. Be mindful of signs of dehydration, such as dark urine, dizziness, or

excessive thirst.

Autumn and Winter Preparation:

- **Layering Clothing:** As temperatures drop, layering clothing helps regulate body temperature and keep your child warm. Choose moisture-wicking base layers, insulating middle layers, and waterproof outer layers for cold, wet conditions. Ensure that your child wears a hat, gloves, and a scarf to protect extremities from the cold.
- **Indoor Activities:** With shorter days and colder weather, indoor activities become more important. Plan engaging indoor activities, such as crafts, games, or reading, to keep your child active and entertained. Ensure that indoor play areas are safe and free from hazards.
- **Home Heating:** Check that your home's heating system is working efficiently and safely. Use space heaters with safety features, such as automatic shut-off, and keep them away from flammable materials. Ensure that carbon monoxide detectors are functioning and have fresh batteries.

Sun Protection and Hydration

Protecting your child from the sun and ensuring proper hydration is crucial for maintaining their health and safety, especially during warmer months or when spending extended periods outdoors.

Sun Protection:

- **Sunscreen:** Use broad-spectrum sunscreen with an SPF of 30 or higher. Apply sunscreen generously to all exposed skin, including areas often missed such as the back of the ears and the tops of the feet. Reapply every two hours, or more frequently if swimming or sweating. Choose a sunscreen that is suitable for your child's skin type and age.
- **Protective Clothing:** Dress your child in lightweight, long-sleeved shirts and long pants made of breathable fabrics that offer UV protection. Look for clothing with built-in UV protection ratings for added safety. A wide-brimmed hat provides shade for the face, ears, and neck.
- **Shade and Timing:** Encourage your child to seek shade, especially during peak sun hours from 10 a.m. to 4 p.m., when UV rays are strongest. Use shaded areas such as umbrellas, canopies, or natural shade from trees to reduce direct sun exposure.
- **Sunglasses:** Choose sunglasses that offer 100% UV protection to shield your child's eyes from harmful rays. Ensure that the sunglasses fit properly and are comfortable to wear.

Hydration:

- **Regular Water Intake:** Encourage your child to drink water regularly, even if they're not feeling thirsty. Provide water with every meal and during play or physical activities. Offer water-rich foods like fruits and vegetables, which also contribute to hydration.
- **Avoid Sugary Drinks:** Limit the intake of sugary drinks and sodas, which can contribute to dehydration and other health issues. Opt for water, milk, or diluted fruit juices as healthier alternatives.
- **Recognizing Dehydration:** Be aware of signs of dehydration, including dark yellow urine, dry mouth, fatigue, and dizziness. If you notice these signs, increase fluid intake and consult a healthcare provider if symptoms persist or worsen.

Cold Weather Care

Cold weather presents specific challenges for keeping your child warm, healthy, and safe. Proper care and preparation can help prevent cold-related health issues and ensure your child remains comfortable during the winter months.

Dressing for Cold Weather:

- **Layering:** Dress your child in layers to provide better insulation and adjust their clothing as needed. Start with a moisture-wicking base layer to keep sweat away from the skin, followed by insulating layers for warmth, and finish with a waterproof, windproof outer layer to protect against the elements.
- **Warm Accessories:** Equip your child with essential winter accessories, including a warm hat that covers the ears, insulated gloves or mittens, and a scarf to protect the neck and face. Ensure that boots are waterproof and insulated to keep feet warm and dry.
- **Avoid Overheating:** While it's important to keep your child warm, be cautious of overheating. Ensure that your child can easily remove layers if they become too warm, and avoid excessive bundling that can restrict movement and cause discomfort.

Preventing Cold-Related Illnesses:

- **Frostbite and Hypothermia:** Be mindful of frostbite and hypothermia, which can occur in extreme cold. Signs of frostbite include numbness, pale or red skin, and blisters. Hypothermia symptoms include shivering, confusion, and drowsiness. If you suspect either condition, seek medical attention immediately and warm the affected areas gradually.
- **Indoor Air Quality:** Maintain good indoor air quality by using a humidifier to prevent dry skin and respiratory discomfort caused by heated indoor air. Ensure that your home is well-ventilated and that heating systems are regularly inspected and maintained.

Safety Tips for Various Seasons

Each season brings unique safety concerns that require specific precautions to protect your child from potential hazards. Being aware of these concerns and taking preventive measures can help ensure your child's safety throughout the year.

Spring Safety:

- **Outdoor Activities:** As the weather warms up, ensure your child is supervised during outdoor activities to prevent accidents and injuries. Check play areas for hazards such as sharp objects or unsafe surfaces. Teach your child about safety rules for biking, skating, or playing near water.
- **Pest Control:** Spring is a time for increased insect activity. Protect your child from insect bites and stings by using insect repellent, wearing appropriate clothing, and avoiding areas with high insect populations. Be cautious of ticks and their potential for carrying diseases like Lyme disease.

Summer Safety:

- **Water Safety:** Supervise your child closely around pools, lakes, or other bodies of water. Teach your child to swim and adhere to water safety rules. Use life jackets for young or inexperienced swimmers and ensure that pool areas are fenced and secure.
- **Heat Safety:** Prevent heat-related illnesses by ensuring your child stays hydrated, avoids prolonged exposure to high temperatures, and takes breaks in cool or shaded areas. Be mindful of symptoms such as heat exhaustion, which can include dizziness, headache, and nausea.

Autumn Safety:

- **Halloween Safety:** For Halloween, ensure your child's costume is safe and visible. Choose costumes that are flame-resistant, fit well to avoid tripping, and include reflective materials for visibility in low-light conditions. Accompany your child during trick-or-treating and inspect candy before consumption.

- **School Safety:** As children return to school, review pedestrian safety and traffic rules. Ensure that your child knows how to cross streets safely, use crosswalks, and stay alert around traffic. Encourage them to follow school safety rules and report any concerns to a trusted adult.

Winter Safety:

- **Snow and Ice:** Be cautious of snow and ice when your child is playing outdoors. Teach them to walk carefully on slippery surfaces and avoid running or roughhousing in icy conditions. Use salt or sand to improve traction on driveways and sidewalks.
- **Emergency Preparedness:** Prepare for winter emergencies by having an emergency kit with essentials like blankets, food, water, and a flashlight. Ensure that your family is familiar with emergency procedures and that your home's heating system is in good working order.

General Safety Tips:

- **Emergency Contacts:** Maintain a list of emergency contacts, including local emergency services, healthcare providers, and family members. Ensure that your child knows how to contact you or another trusted adult in case of an emergency.
- **Safety Education:** Continuously educate your child about safety rules and practices appropriate for each season. Reinforce the importance of following safety guidelines and being aware of their surroundings.

TEN

BEHAVIOURAL GUIDANCE

Positive Reinforcement Techniques

Positive reinforcement is a powerful tool for encouraging desired behaviours and fostering a positive relationship between parents and children. By focusing on rewarding good behaviour rather than merely punishing misbehaviour, you can help your child develop self-discipline and a positive outlook.

Understanding Positive Reinforcement:

- **Definition and Purpose:** Positive reinforcement involves offering rewards or incentives to encourage desired behaviours. This can include verbal praise, physical affection, or tangible rewards like stickers or extra playtime. The goal is to reinforce behaviours you want to see more frequently, making them more likely to recur.
- **Immediate and Specific Praise:** Provide immediate and specific feedback when your child displays positive behaviour. For example, instead of a general "good job," say, "I really like how you cleaned up your toys without being asked." Specific praise helps your child understand exactly what behaviour is being rewarded and reinforces it more effectively.

Types of Reinforcement:

- **Verbal Praise:** Simple and effective, verbal praise acknowledges your child's efforts and accomplishments. Use encouraging words and a positive tone to make your child feel valued and appreciated. For example, "I'm so proud of how you finished your homework on your own today."

- **Physical Rewards:** Hugs, high-fives, and other forms of physical affection can be powerful reinforcers. These actions convey warmth and approval, reinforcing your child's sense of connection and accomplishment.
- **Tangible Rewards:** Occasionally using tangible rewards, such as stickers, tokens, or small treats, can be motivating for children. Be mindful to use these rewards sparingly to avoid creating an expectation that every good behaviour will be rewarded with a physical item.
- **Privileges and Special Activities:** Offering additional privileges or special activities as a reward can be effective. For example, allowing your child to choose a movie to watch or have an extra half-hour of playtime can be motivating and enjoyable.

Consistency and Fairness:

- **Consistent Application:** Apply positive reinforcement consistently to ensure your child understands that the rewards are linked to specific behaviours. Inconsistent reinforcement can lead to confusion and reduce the effectiveness of the technique.
- **Fairness and Equity:** Ensure that reinforcement is fair and equitable. Avoid giving rewards based on favouritism or arbitrary criteria. Consistent and fair application of rewards helps maintain trust and encourages positive behaviour.

Setting Boundaries and Rules

Setting clear boundaries and rules is essential for creating a structured and safe environment for your child. Well-defined expectations help children understand acceptable behaviour and the consequences of their actions.

Establishing Clear Rules:

- **Define Expectations:** Clearly define the rules and expectations for behaviour in your household. Use simple and age-appropriate language that your child can easily understand. For example, "No jumping on the furniture" or "Please use your indoor voice."
- **Involve Your Child:** Involving your child in the rule-setting process can increase their sense of ownership and adherence. Discuss the reasons for the rules and allow your child to contribute their thoughts. This collaborative approach helps your child feel respected and engaged.

Consistent Enforcement:

- **Apply Rules Consistently:** Consistency is key to effective discipline. Apply rules consistently to avoid confusion and ensure that your child understands the consequences of breaking them. Inconsistent enforcement can lead to frustration and undermine the effectiveness of the rules.
- **Follow Through with Consequences:** Implement appropriate consequences for rule violations as outlined in your established guidelines. Consequences should be logical and related to the behaviour, such as losing screen time for not completing homework. Follow through with consequences to reinforce the importance of adhering to rules.

Positive Discipline Techniques:

- **Focus on Behaviour, Not Character:** Address specific behaviours rather than labelling your child's character. For example, instead of saying "You're bad," focus on the behaviour by saying, "Throwing toys is not acceptable." This approach helps your child understand that their actions, not their character, are being addressed.

- **Encourage Problem-Solving:** Involve your child in finding solutions to behavior-related issues. Encourage them to think about alternative actions and the potential consequences of their choices. This approach promotes critical thinking and self-regulation.

Adjusting Rules as Needed:

- **Developmental Considerations:** Adjust rules and expectations based on your child's developmental stage and individual needs. As your child grows, their understanding and abilities will evolve, requiring modifications to rules and boundaries.
- **Flexibility and Adaptation:** Be open to revising rules and boundaries as needed. Changes in family circumstances, such as moving to a new home or starting school, may necessitate adjustments to the rules. Communicate these changes clearly to your child and involve them in the discussion.

Conflict Resolution and Problem-Solving

Teaching your child effective conflict resolution and problem-solving skills is crucial for their social and emotional development. These skills help children navigate interpersonal challenges and develop positive relationships with others.

Teaching Conflict Resolution Skills:

- **Modelling behaviour:** Demonstrate effective conflict resolution techniques by modelling calm and respectful interactions with others. Show your child how to handle disagreements constructively and respectfully. Your behaviour sets an example for how they should approach conflicts.
- **Encouraging Communication:** Teach your child to express their feelings and concerns calmly and respectfully. Encourage open communication by listening to their perspective and validating their emotions. Use "I" statements, such as "I feel frustrated when..." to express feelings without blaming.
- **Finding Common Ground:** Help your child identify common ground and shared interests when resolving conflicts. Encourage them to work together to find mutually acceptable solutions. This approach fosters cooperation and empathy.

Problem-Solving Strategies:

- **Identifying the Problem:** Guide your child in clearly identifying the problem or challenge they are facing. Encourage them to describe the situation and their feelings about it. Understanding the problem is the first step in finding an effective solution.
- **Brainstorming Solutions:** Involve your child in brainstorming potential solutions to the problem. Encourage creativity and consider a range of options. Discuss the pros and cons of each solution and help your child evaluate which one might be the most effective.
- **Implementing and Reviewing Solutions:** Support your child in implementing the chosen solution and reviewing its effectiveness. Discuss what worked well and what could be improved. This reflective process helps your child learn from their experiences and refine their

problem-solving skills.

Building Self-Esteem and Confidence

Building self-esteem and confidence is essential for your child's emotional well-being and success. A positive self-image helps children navigate challenges, set goals, and develop resilience.

Encouraging a Positive Self-Image:

- **Affirming Strengths:** Focus on your child's strengths and accomplishments. Offer praise and encouragement for their efforts, skills, and positive attributes. Acknowledge their unique talents and abilities, and help them recognize their value.
- **Setting Realistic Goals:** Help your child set achievable goals and celebrate their progress. Setting and reaching goals builds confidence and a sense of accomplishment. Break larger goals into smaller, manageable steps to ensure success and maintain motivation.

Providing Support and Encouragement:

- **Emphasizing Effort and Persistence:** Reinforce the importance of effort and persistence rather than just outcomes. Encourage your child to try their best and learn from setbacks. Praising their perseverance helps build resilience and a growth mindset.
- **Offering Opportunities for Success:** Provide opportunities for your child to succeed and experience positive outcomes. Engage them in activities that align with their interests and strengths, and support their participation in hobbies, sports, or academic pursuits.

Fostering Independence and Autonomy:

- **Encouraging Decision-Making:** Allow your child to make decisions and take responsibility for their actions. Offer choices and let them experience the consequences of their decisions. This practice helps build confidence and independence.
- **Supporting Self-Expression:** Encourage your child to express their thoughts, feelings, and opinions. Validate their emotions and provide a supportive environment where they feel comfortable sharing their ideas. Self-expression fosters a strong sense of self-worth.

Building a Positive Environment:

- **Creating a Supportive Atmosphere:** Foster a positive and supportive home environment where your child feels valued and encouraged. Provide a safe space for them to explore their interests, take risks, and learn from their experiences.
- **Celebrating Achievements:** Celebrate your child's achievements, both big and small. Recognize their efforts and successes with enthusiasm and pride. Celebrations reinforce their sense of accomplishment and motivate them to continue pursuing their goals.

ELEVEN

SPECIAL NEEDS AND INCLUSIVITY

Recognizing and Supporting Special Needs

Understanding and addressing special needs requires a compassionate and informed approach. Early recognition and appropriate support can significantly impact a child's development and quality of life.

Identifying Special Needs:

- **Signs and Symptoms:** Special needs can manifest in various ways, including developmental delays, learning disabilities, physical disabilities, or behavioural issues. Common signs may include difficulties with speech or language, challenges with motor skills, problems with attention or focus, and struggles with social interactions. Be observant of any significant differences from typical developmental milestones and consult professionals for a comprehensive evaluation if concerns arise.
- **Early Intervention:** Early identification of special needs is crucial for effective intervention. If you suspect your child may have special needs, seek professional evaluation from a paediatrician, psychologist, or other specialists. Early intervention services, such as speech therapy, occupational therapy, or special education programs, can provide targeted support and help your child reach their full potential.

Providing Support:

- **Individualized Approach:** Tailor your support to your child's unique needs. This may involve creating individualized education plans (IEPs) or personalized therapy goals based on their specific strengths and challenges. Collaborate with professionals to develop strategies and interventions that are best suited to your child's needs.
- **Creating a Supportive Environment:** Foster a nurturing and supportive home environment that encourages your child's growth and development. This includes providing a structured routine, clear expectations, and positive reinforcement. Adapt your approach as needed to accommodate your child's specific requirements.
- **Encouraging Independence:** Promote your child's independence by gradually increasing their responsibilities and opportunities for self-expression. Encourage them to participate in activities and make choices that align with their abilities. Support their efforts while providing guidance and assistance when needed.

Resources and Support Systems

Accessing appropriate resources and support systems can provide valuable assistance in addressing your child's special needs and enhancing their development.

Educational Resources:

- **Special Education Services:** Explore special education services available through local schools or educational institutions. These services may include individualized instruction, resource rooms, or specialized programs designed to meet your child's needs. Work with educators to develop and implement an effective individualized education plan (IEP) or 504 plan.
- **Therapeutic Services:** Identify therapeutic services such as speech therapy, occupational therapy, or physical therapy that can support your child's development. These services can address specific challenges and provide targeted interventions to improve skills and functioning.

Support Organizations and Networks:

- **Parent Support Groups:** Connect with parent support groups or organizations that focus on special needs. These groups can offer emotional support, practical advice, and resources for navigating challenges. Engaging with others who have similar experiences can provide valuable insights and a sense of community.
- **Online Resources:** Utilize online resources, including websites, forums, and social media groups, to access information and support related to special needs. Many organizations offer valuable resources, including articles, webinars, and toolkits designed to assist parents and caregivers.

Professional Support:

- **Healthcare Providers:** Maintain open communication with your child's healthcare providers, including paediatricians, specialists, and therapists. Regular check-ins and consultations can help monitor progress, address concerns, and adjust interventions as needed.

- **Advocacy Services:** Consider seeking advocacy services to support your child's educational and medical needs. Advocates can assist with navigating school systems, securing necessary services, and addressing any challenges or barriers you may encounter.

Promoting Inclusivity and Empathy

Creating an inclusive environment and fostering empathy helps children with special needs feel valued and supported. Encouraging inclusivity benefits all children by promoting understanding and acceptance.

Fostering Inclusivity:

- **Inclusive Education:** Advocate for inclusive educational practices that allow children with special needs to participate fully in mainstream classrooms. Inclusive education promotes diversity and provides opportunities for all students to learn and grow together. Support teachers and schools in implementing inclusive strategies and accommodations.
- **Community Activities:** Encourage participation in community activities, clubs, and extracurricular programs that welcome children with special needs. Inclusive programs provide opportunities for social interaction and skill development while promoting acceptance and understanding among peers.

Teaching Empathy and Respect:

- **Modelling Empathy:** Demonstrate empathy and respect in your interactions with others. Show kindness, understanding, and patience in your behaviour, and encourage your child to do the same. Discuss the importance of treating others with compassion and recognizing the value of each individual's unique qualities.
- **Educational Resources:** Utilize books, videos, and other educational resources that address special needs and promote empathy. Age-appropriate materials can help children understand and appreciate differences, fostering a more inclusive and supportive attitude.

Addressing Bullying and Discrimination:

- **Promoting Awareness:** Educate your child about bullying and discrimination, emphasizing the importance of standing up against these behaviours. Encourage open dialogue about how to address bullying and seek support if they or others experience discrimination or exclusion.

- **Creating a Supportive Environment:** Work with schools and community organizations to create a supportive environment where all children feel safe and included. Support initiatives that promote diversity, equity, and inclusion, and advocate for policies and practices that address bullying and discrimination.

Understanding Developmental Delays

Developmental delays refer to slower-than-typical progress in areas such as speech, motor skills, or social-emotional development. Early identification and intervention are essential for addressing developmental delays and supporting your child's growth.

Identifying Developmental Delays:

- **Common Delays:** Developmental delays can affect various areas, including speech and language, motor skills, cognitive abilities, and social-emotional development. Signs may include delayed speech, difficulty with coordination, challenges in problem-solving, or struggles with forming relationships.
- **Assessment and Diagnosis:** If you suspect a developmental delay, seek a comprehensive evaluation from a healthcare provider or specialist. Assessments may include developmental screenings, diagnostic tests, and observations to determine the nature and extent of the delay.

Intervening Early:

- **Early Intervention Services:** Early intervention services can provide targeted support to address developmental delays. Services may include speech therapy, occupational therapy, physical therapy, or specialized educational programs. Early intervention helps improve outcomes and supports your child's overall development.
- **Individualized Approach:** Develop an individualized plan to address your child's specific needs. Collaborate with professionals to set goals and implement strategies that target the areas of delay. Regularly review and adjust the plan based on your child's progress.

Supporting Your Child:

- **Creating a Nurturing Environment:** Provide a supportive and nurturing environment that encourages your child's development. Use positive reinforcement, establish consistent routines, and offer opportunities for skill-building activities. Celebrate your child's progress and efforts, regardless of the pace of development.

- **Parent Education and Support:** Educate yourself about developmental delays and seek support from professionals and parent groups. Understanding your child's needs and accessing resources can empower you to advocate effectively and provide the best support for your child.

Promoting a Positive Outlook:

- **Encouraging Growth and Development:** Focus on your child's strengths and achievements, and maintain a positive outlook. Encourage perseverance and resilience, and support your child in overcoming challenges. A positive attitude fosters confidence and motivation in your child.
- **Building Self-Esteem:** Support your child's self-esteem by recognizing their efforts and celebrating their successes. Avoid comparisons with peers and emphasize their unique qualities and abilities. Building self-esteem helps your child develop a strong sense of self-worth and confidence.

TWELVE

PARENTAL SELF-CARE

Importance of Maternal Health and Wellbeing

Maintaining maternal health and well-being is crucial for both the mother and her family. A healthy and well-cared-for mother is better equipped to provide nurturing care and support to her child.

Physical Health:

- **Regular Check-ups:** Regular medical check-ups are essential for monitoring physical health. These include routine visits to a primary care physician, gynaecologist, and any specialists needed. Regular screenings and preventive care can help manage health conditions and promote overall wellness.
- **Exercise and Nutrition:** Incorporate regular physical activity into your routine. Exercise improves physical fitness, boosts energy levels, and supports mental health. Complement this with a balanced diet rich in essential nutrients to support overall health and energy.
- **Adequate Rest:** Prioritize sufficient sleep and rest. Proper rest is vital for physical recovery, cognitive function, and emotional stability. Create a consistent sleep routine and find moments throughout the day for relaxation and rejuvenation.

Mental and Emotional Health:

- **Self-awareness:** Pay attention to your mental and emotional state. Recognize signs of stress, anxiety, or depression, and seek professional help if needed. Regular self-reflection and mindfulness can help manage emotional well-being.

- **Self-compassion:** Practice self-compassion and avoid self-criticism. Acknowledge that parenting is challenging and allow yourself to make mistakes. Being kind to yourself can improve resilience and overall well-being.

Work-Life Balance:

- **Setting Boundaries:** Establish clear boundaries between work and family life. Set specific times for work and family activities, and avoid letting work encroach on family time. Creating boundaries helps reduce stress and improve quality time with family.
- **Prioritizing Self-Care:** Schedule regular self-care activities that rejuvenate and relax you. Whether it's reading a book, taking a walk, or engaging in a hobby, self-care is crucial for maintaining balance and well-being.

Stress Management Techniques

Effectively managing stress is essential for maintaining both physical and mental health. Implementing stress management techniques can help you cope with the demands of parenting and daily life.

Identifying Stressors:

- **Recognizing Triggers:** Identify the sources of stress in your life, whether they are related to work, parenting, or personal responsibilities. Understanding your stressors can help you develop strategies to manage or mitigate them.
- **Monitoring Stress Levels:** Pay attention to your stress levels and physical symptoms such as headaches, fatigue, or irritability. Regular self-assessment can help you address stress before it becomes overwhelming.

Stress Reduction Techniques:

- **Deep Breathing and Relaxation:** Practice deep breathing exercises and relaxation techniques to calm your mind and body. Techniques such as diaphragmatic breathing, progressive muscle relaxation, and guided imagery can help reduce stress and promote relaxation.
- **Mindfulness and Meditation:** Incorporate mindfulness and meditation into your daily routine. Mindfulness practices, such as mindful breathing and body scans, can help you stay present and reduce anxiety. Meditation can provide a sense of calm and improve emotional resilience.
- **Physical Activity:** Engage in regular physical exercise to reduce stress and improve mood. Activities such as walking, jogging, yoga, or dancing can help release endorphins and alleviate tension.

Time Management and Organization:

- **Prioritizing Tasks:** Use time management techniques to prioritize tasks and manage your workload. Create a daily or weekly schedule to organize your responsibilities and allocate time for self-care and relaxation.

- **Setting Realistic Goals:** Set achievable goals and break tasks into smaller, manageable steps. Avoid overloading yourself with unrealistic expectations and allow for flexibility in your plans.

Seeking Professional Support:

- **Therapy and Counselling:** Consider seeking therapy or counselling if stress becomes overwhelming. Mental health professionals can provide guidance, coping strategies, and emotional support to help you manage stress effectively.
- **Support Groups:** Join support groups or online communities where you can share experiences and receive support from others who are going through similar challenges. Connecting with others can provide valuable insights and encouragement.

Building a Support Network

A strong support network is crucial for maintaining well-being and managing the challenges of parenting. Building and nurturing relationships with supportive individuals can provide emotional and practical assistance.

Identifying Sources of Support:

- **Family and Friends:** Cultivate relationships with family and friends who can offer emotional support, practical help, and encouragement. Share your experiences and seek their advice or assistance when needed.
- **Parenting Groups:** Join local or online parenting groups to connect with other parents. These groups can provide valuable advice, support, and a sense of community. Engaging with others who share similar experiences can be comforting and informative.

Seeking Professional Help:

- **Healthcare Providers:** Build relationships with healthcare providers who can offer guidance and support for both your and your child's needs. Regular communication with doctors, therapists, and counsellors can provide essential support and resources.
- **Childcare Providers:** Develop a positive relationship with childcare providers or educators. Effective communication and collaboration with these professionals can ensure that your child's needs are met and provide you with additional support.

Balancing Relationships:

- **Maintaining Connections:** Make an effort to stay connected with your support network, even during busy or stressful times. Regular communication, whether through phone calls, texts, or in-person visits, helps maintain strong relationships and support systems.
- **Mutual Support:** Offer support to others in your network as well. Building reciprocal relationships where you both give and receive support can strengthen your connections and foster a sense of community.

Balancing Work and Family Life

Finding a balance between work and family life is essential for maintaining well-being and ensuring that both personal and professional responsibilities are managed effectively.

Establishing Priorities:

- **Setting Goals:** Define your priorities and set goals for both work and family life. Consider what is most important to you and allocate time and energy accordingly. Clear goals help you stay focused and manage your responsibilities effectively.
- **Creating a Schedule:** Develop a structured schedule that balances work commitments with family time. Use tools such as calendars or planners to organize your daily activities and ensure that you have dedicated time for family and self-care.

Flexible Work Arrangements:

- **Negotiating Flexibility:** Explore flexible work arrangements with your employer, such as telecommuting, flexible hours, or job sharing. Flexibility can help you manage work and family responsibilities more effectively and reduce stress.
- **Setting Boundaries:** Establish clear boundaries between work and family time. Avoid bringing work home or allowing work-related issues to interfere with family time. Create a designated workspace if working from home to maintain separation between work and personal life.

Quality Time with Family:

- **Prioritizing Family Activities:** Schedule regular family activities and quality time together. Engage in activities that strengthen family bonds and create positive memories. Prioritizing family time helps ensure that you maintain strong connections with your loved ones.
- **Effective Communication:** Communicate openly with your family about your work schedule and commitments. Share your goals and any challenges you may be facing. Open communication fosters understanding and support from family members.

Self-Care and Recharge:

- **Taking Breaks:** Make time for regular breaks and self-care to recharge and avoid burnout. Prioritize activities that help you relax and rejuvenate, such as exercise, hobbies, or spending time with friends.
- **Seeking Help When Needed:** Don't hesitate to seek help or delegate tasks when needed. Whether it's asking for assistance from family members, hiring help, or seeking professional support, getting help can alleviate stress and improve work-life balance.

THIRTEEN

CULTURAL AND ETHICAL VALUES

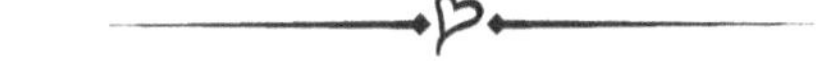

Teaching Cultural Heritage and Traditions

Instilling a sense of cultural heritage and traditions in children enriches their identity and helps them connect with their roots. Understanding one's culture fosters a sense of belonging and pride, while traditions provide a framework for values and community.

Understanding Cultural Heritage:

- **Exploring Family Background:** Share stories about your family's cultural background and history with your children. Discuss traditions, customs, and significant events that have shaped your family's heritage. Personal stories and experiences make cultural heritage more relatable and meaningful.
- **Cultural Practices:** Introduce your children to cultural practices, such as traditional foods, festivals, clothing, and rituals. Involve them in cultural activities and celebrations, explaining their significance and how they connect to your family's history and identity.

Celebrating Traditions:

- **Incorporating Traditions:** Make cultural traditions a regular part of your family life. Celebrate traditional holidays and events, and incorporate cultural practices into daily routines where possible. This helps children experience and appreciate their heritage in a meaningful way.

- **Creating New Traditions:** In addition to celebrating established traditions, consider creating new family traditions that blend cultural practices with modern life. This can include unique ways of celebrating holidays, family rituals, or special occasions that reflect both cultural heritage and contemporary values.

Educating About Cultural Diversity:

- **Books and Media:** Use books, movies, and educational materials that explore different cultures and traditions. Reading stories and watching media from diverse backgrounds can broaden your child's understanding and appreciation of various cultures.
- **Cultural Events and Experiences:** Attend cultural events, festivals, and exhibitions in your community. Engaging in activities that showcase different cultures provides practical experiences and fosters a deeper connection to cultural diversity.

Instilling Ethical and Moral Values

Teaching ethical and moral values helps children develop a strong sense of right and wrong, guiding their behaviour and decisions. Ethical values form the foundation of character development and interpersonal relationships.

Core Ethical Values:

- **Honesty and Integrity:** Emphasize the importance of honesty and integrity in everyday situations. Teach children to value truthfulness, keep promises, and act with integrity. Model these behaviours in your own actions to reinforce their significance.
- **Respect and Kindness:** Foster a sense of respect and kindness towards others. Encourage children to treat people with empathy, fairness, and compassion. Discuss the importance of understanding different perspectives and showing respect for others' feelings and opinions.
- **Responsibility and Accountability:** Teach children to take responsibility for their actions and decisions. Encourage them to be accountable for their behaviour, make amends when necessary, and learn from their mistakes. Instilling a sense of responsibility helps build self-discipline and reliability.

Moral Decision-Making:

- **Discussing Moral Dilemmas:** Engage in discussions about moral dilemmas and ethical situations relevant to their age. Use real-life scenarios or stories to explore various perspectives and decision-making processes. Encourage critical thinking and ethical reasoning.
- **Encouraging Reflection:** Help children reflect on their actions and their impact on others. Discuss the consequences of different choices and guide them in evaluating the ethical aspects of their decisions. Reflection promotes self-awareness and moral growth.

Role Modeling:

- **Leading by Example:** Demonstrate ethical behavior through your own actions. Children learn a great deal from observing adults, so model the values you wish to instil. Show how you handle ethical dilemmas and make moral decisions in your daily life.

- **Positive Reinforcement:** Acknowledge and praise ethical behavior when you observe it. Positive reinforcement encourages children to continue making morally sound choices and reinforces the importance of ethical values.

Encouraging Respect and Tolerance

Promoting respect and tolerance helps children develop an appreciation for diversity and fosters harmonious relationships. These values are crucial for creating an inclusive and supportive environment.

Teaching Respect:

- **Respect for Others:** Teach children to respect people regardless of their differences, including race, ethnicity, religion, or socioeconomic status. Discuss the importance of treating everyone with dignity and consideration.
- **Respect for Property and Boundaries:** Emphasize the importance of respecting personal property and boundaries. Teach children to ask for permission before using others' belongings and to be mindful of others' personal space.

Promoting Tolerance:

- **Understanding Differences:** Encourage children to learn about and understand different cultures, beliefs, and lifestyles. Provide opportunities for them to interact with people from diverse backgrounds and participate in activities that celebrate diversity.
- **Addressing Prejudice:** Address any prejudiced or discriminatory attitudes that may arise. Have open and honest conversations about stereotypes and biases, and provide guidance on how to challenge and overcome these attitudes.

Celebrating Diversity

Celebrating diversity enriches children's understanding of the world and fosters an appreciation for differences. Encouraging a diverse and inclusive mindset promotes a more harmonious and accepting society.

Exposure to Diversity:

- **Diverse Environments:** Create opportunities for your children to engage with diverse environments and experiences. This can include participating in multicultural events, visiting diverse neighbourhoods, or interacting with individuals from various backgrounds.
- **Educational Materials:** Use educational resources that reflect diverse cultures and perspectives. Books, documentaries, and educational programs that highlight different experiences and viewpoints help children appreciate and celebrate diversity.

Inclusive Activities:

- **Celebrating Diverse Holidays:** Include a variety of cultural and religious holidays in your family celebrations. This not only exposes children to different traditions but also teaches them the value of inclusivity and respect for all cultures.
- **Encouraging Open Dialogue:** Foster an environment where children feel comfortable discussing diversity and asking questions. Encourage open dialogue about different cultures, beliefs, and experiences, and address any misconceptions or stereotypes.

Modelling Inclusivity:

- **Demonstrating Acceptance:** Show acceptance and appreciation for diverse cultures and individuals in your own actions and interactions. Model inclusive behaviour and attitudes, and demonstrate how to celebrate and honour diversity in everyday life.
- **Community Involvement:** Engage in community activities that promote diversity and inclusion. Support organizations and initiatives that work towards fostering an inclusive society and encourage your children to participate in these efforts.

FOURTEEN

TECHNOLOGY AND MODERN PARENTING

Navigating the Digital World

In today's digital age, navigating the digital world is a crucial aspect of parenting. Understanding the impact of technology on children and guiding them in their digital experiences are essential for fostering healthy technology use.

Understanding Technology's Impact:

- **Positive Effects:** Technology can offer significant benefits, such as educational opportunities, access to information, and the ability to connect with others. Educational tools and resources can enhance learning, while communication platforms can help maintain relationships with family and friends.
- **Potential Risks:** Technology use can also pose risks, including exposure to inappropriate content, potential addiction, and the impact on physical and mental health. Understanding these risks helps in developing strategies to manage and mitigate them effectively.

Age-Appropriate Technology Use:

- **Developmental Considerations:** Tailor technology use to your child's age and developmental stage. Younger children benefit from limited screen time and high-quality educational content, while older children can handle more complex interactions and responsibilities with technology.

- **Guidelines for Use:** Establish age-appropriate guidelines for technology use. This includes setting limits on screen time, selecting suitable content, and supervising your child's online activities. Adapt these guidelines as your child grows and technology evolves.

Encouraging Balanced Technology Use:

- **Promoting Offline Activities:** Encourage participation in offline activities such as physical exercise, outdoor play, and creative pursuits. A balanced approach to technology ensures that children engage in a variety of experiences that support their overall development.
- **Family Time:** Use technology as a tool for family engagement. Plan family activities that incorporate technology in a positive way, such as playing educational games together or exploring interactive learning experiences.

Educational Apps and Resources

Educational apps and resources can support and enhance your child's learning experiences. Selecting high-quality educational tools and integrating them into your child's routine can provide valuable learning opportunities.

Selecting Quality Apps:

- **Criteria for Selection:** Choose educational apps that are age-appropriate, engaging, and aligned with your child's learning needs. Look for apps that offer interactive content, promote critical thinking, and provide opportunities for skill development.
- **Reviews and Recommendations:** Utilize reviews, recommendations, and ratings from educational experts and other parents to evaluate app quality. Many educational apps offer trial versions or free content, allowing you to assess their suitability before making a commitment.

Integrating Apps into Learning:

- **Setting Goals:** Incorporate educational apps into your child's learning routine with specific goals in mind. Use apps to reinforce concepts learned in school, explore new topics, or support areas where your child may need additional practice.
- **Balancing Screen Time:** Ensure that the use of educational apps is balanced with other learning activities. Combine screen time with hands-on learning experiences, reading, and creative activities to provide a well-rounded educational experience.

Online Safety and Cyber Bullying

Ensuring online safety and addressing cyberbullying are critical aspects of modern parenting. Protecting your child from online dangers and fostering a positive digital environment is essential for their well-being.

Online Safety Measures:

- **Setting Privacy Settings:** Teach your child how to set privacy settings on social media and other online platforms. Ensure that their personal information is protected and that they understand the importance of controlling who can view their content.
- **Safe Online Practices:** Educate your child about safe online practices, such as avoiding sharing personal information, recognizing phishing attempts, and reporting suspicious activity. Encourage them to use strong passwords and avoid engaging with unknown individuals online.

Addressing Cyberbullying:

- **Recognizing Signs:** Be aware of signs that your child may be experiencing cyberbullying, such as changes in behaviour, withdrawal from online activities, or unexplained distress. Open communication and a supportive approach are crucial in addressing these issues.
- **Providing Support:** Offer emotional support and guidance if your child encounters cyberbullying. Encourage them to report the behaviour to the platform and seek help from school officials or mental health professionals if needed. Foster an environment where your child feels safe and empowered to discuss their online experiences.

Setting Boundaries with Technology

Establishing clear boundaries with technology helps manage its impact on your child's life and ensures balanced and healthy technology use.

Establishing Screen Time Limits:

- **Creating a Schedule:** Develop a screen time schedule that outlines when and how long your child can use technology. Balance screen time with other activities, such as homework, physical exercise, and family interactions. Adjust the schedule as needed based on your child's age and needs.
- **Enforcing Limits:** Be consistent in enforcing screen time limits. Use tools such as parental controls and apps that track screen time to help manage and monitor usage. Discuss the reasons for these limits with your child to promote understanding and cooperation.

Defining Technology-Free Zones:

- **Designating Areas:** Establish technology-free zones in your home, such as the dining area or bedrooms. Creating spaces where technology is not allowed encourages face-to-face interactions and ensures that technology does not interfere with important activities like meals and sleep.
- **Encouraging Offline Activities:** Promote technology-free activities, such as family games, outdoor play, and creative projects. Engaging in activities that do not involve screens helps children develop diverse skills and interests.

Monitoring and Supervision:

- **Active Supervision:** Actively supervise your child's technology use, especially with younger children. Monitor the content they access, the platforms they use, and their interactions online. Open dialogue about their online activities helps build trust and ensures safe technology use.
- **Setting a Positive Example:** Model responsible technology use for your child. Demonstrate how to balance screen time with other activities and maintain healthy technology habits. Your behaviour sets an example for

your child and reinforces the importance of responsible technology use.

FIFTEEN
CONCLUSION

Recap of Key Takeaways

In concluding this guidebook, it's essential to recap the core concepts and strategies that have been discussed throughout each chapter. This summary will reinforce the foundational principles of child nourishment and development, highlighting key takeaways for mothers to apply in their parenting journey.

Holistic Approach to Child Development:

- **Physical Health:** Emphasizing the importance of balanced nutrition, regular exercise, and adequate sleep is crucial for fostering healthy physical development. Establishing routines and promoting a well-rounded diet support children's growth and overall well-being.
- **Cognitive Growth:** Stimulating cognitive development through play, reading, puzzles, and encouraging curiosity helps enhance problem-solving skills, memory, and language acquisition. Engaging children in educational activities supports their intellectual growth and prepares them for future learning experiences.
- **Emotional and Social Development:** Understanding and managing emotions, building social skills, and encouraging positive behavior are vital for emotional resilience and healthy social interactions. Effective strategies for handling tantrums and discipline contribute to a nurturing and supportive environment.
- **Educational Development:** Exploring early childhood education options, preparing for school, supporting homework habits, and fostering a love for learning lay the groundwork for academic success and lifelong learning. Encouraging curiosity and a positive attitude

towards education helps children thrive academically and personally.

- **Habits and Routines:** Establishing daily routines, maintaining consistency, creating a positive home environment, and balancing screen time are key to providing structure and stability. These practices promote a sense of security and support overall family well-being.
- **Seasonal Protection and Safety:** Preparing for different seasons, ensuring sun protection and hydration, caring for cold weather, and implementing safety tips for various seasons help safeguard children's health and well-being throughout the year.
- **Behavioural Guidance:** Using positive reinforcement, setting boundaries, resolving conflicts, and building self-esteem are essential for guiding behavior and fostering a positive self-image. These strategies help children develop appropriate behaviors and strong interpersonal skills.
- **Special Needs and Inclusivity:** Recognizing and supporting special needs, accessing resources and support systems, promoting inclusivity, and understanding developmental delays ensure that all children receive the care and support they need to thrive.
- **Parental Self-Care:** Prioritizing maternal health, managing stress, building a support network, and balancing work and family life are crucial for maintaining overall well-being. Self-care practices enable mothers to provide the best support for their children while maintaining their own health and happiness.
- **Cultural and Ethical Values:** Teaching cultural heritage, instilling ethical values, encouraging respect and tolerance, and celebrating diversity enrich children's understanding of the world and promote a sense of identity and empathy.
- **Technology and Modern Parenting:** Navigating the digital world, utilizing educational apps, ensuring online safety, and setting boundaries with technology are essential for managing technology's impact on children. A balanced approach to technology use supports healthy development and engagement.

Encouraging Lifelong Learning

Fostering a love for lifelong learning is a crucial aspect of nurturing a child's growth and development. Encouraging curiosity and a passion for learning helps children remain engaged and motivated throughout their lives.

Modeling a Love for Learning:

- **Demonstrating Enthusiasm:** Show enthusiasm for learning new things and pursuing personal interests. Your passion for learning sets a positive example and inspires children to value education and intellectual curiosity.
- **Pursuing Interests:** Engage in hobbies and activities that interest you. Share your experiences with your child and involve them in your learning journey. This can include exploring new skills, attending workshops, or reading about topics of interest.

Creating a Learning-Friendly Environment:

- **Encouraging Curiosity:** Foster an environment where questions are welcomed and exploration is encouraged. Provide resources such as books, educational toys, and access to learning opportunities that spark curiosity and inspire creativity.
- **Supporting Educational Goals:** Help your child set and achieve educational goals. Provide guidance and support as they pursue academic interests, participate in extracurricular activities, and explore new subjects. Celebrate their achievements and encourage them to continue learning.

Promoting Continuous Growth:

- **Lifelong Learning Mindset:** Instil the belief that learning is a lifelong journey. Encourage your child to seek out new knowledge, embrace challenges, and view mistakes as opportunities for growth. A growth mindset fosters resilience and a positive attitude towards learning.
- **Accessing Resources:** Explore various resources to support ongoing learning. This can include online courses, community programs,

educational apps, and libraries. Providing access to diverse learning resources enhances opportunities for continued growth and development.

Encouraging Exploration and Creativity:

- **Exploring Interests:** Encourage your child to explore a variety of interests and activities. Allow them to experiment with different hobbies, subjects, and creative outlets. Exploration helps children discover their passions and develop a well-rounded set of skills.
- **Fostering Creativity:** Support creative expression through art, music, writing, and other forms of creativity. Creative activities enhance problem-solving skills, self-expression, and cognitive development. Provide opportunities for your child to experiment and showcase their creative work.

Final Thoughts and Encouragement for Mothers

As this guidebook concludes, it's important to offer final thoughts and encouragement to mothers, acknowledging the challenges and celebrating the joys of parenting.

Embracing the Parenting Journey:

- **Acknowledging Challenges:** Parenting is a journey filled with both challenges and rewards. Embrace the ups and downs with patience and resilience. Recognize that it's okay to seek help, make mistakes, and continuously learn and grow as a parent.
- **Celebrating Achievements:** Celebrate the milestones and achievements of your child and yourself. Each step forward, no matter how small, is a testament to your dedication and love. Take pride in the positive impact you have on your child's life.

Seeking Support and Community:

- **Building Connections:** Connect with other parents, support groups, and community resources. Sharing experiences and seeking advice from others can provide valuable insights and emotional support. Building a strong support network enriches your parenting experience.
- **Accessing Resources:** Utilize available resources, such as parenting books, workshops, and online communities, to enhance your parenting skills and knowledge. Continued learning and access to support can help you navigate the complexities of parenting with confidence.

Prioritizing Self-Care:

- **Taking Care of Yourself:** Prioritize your well-being and self-care. Ensure that you are taking time for yourself, managing stress, and maintaining a healthy work-life balance. Your well-being directly impacts your ability to care for your child effectively.
- **Finding Joy in Parenting:** Embrace the joy and fulfillment that come with parenting. Cherish the moments of connection, laughter, and love with your child. Finding joy in the everyday experiences of parenting enhances your overall satisfaction and strengthens your bond with your

child.

Encouraging Growth and Development:

- **Supporting Your Child's Journey:** Continue to support and nurture your child's growth and development. Provide guidance, encouragement, and opportunities for them to explore their interests and reach their potential. Your involvement and support are the key to their success and happiness.
- **Embracing the Future:** Look forward to the future with optimism and hope. Parenting is a continuous journey of growth and discovery. Embrace the future with confidence, knowing that your efforts and dedication are shaping a positive and promising path for your child.

May you find strength, joy, and wisdom in every step of motherhood, and may your love be the guiding light that shapes a beautiful future for your child.

www.ingramcontent.com/pod-product-compliance
Lightning Source LLC
LaVergne TN
LVHW041110150826
845673LV00007B/2004

* 9 7 9 8 8 9 6 1 0 2 4 0 3 *